Katy

Sequel to *Alias Pandemonium*

Jennette Gahlot

This is a work of fiction. Any names and so forth are a creation of the author's imagination and should not be construed at real.

DEDICATION

To my sisters.

Arkansas U.S. Deputy Marshal Stories

Alias Pandemonium

Katy

Mayhem and Mischief (coming 2017)

Children's Books

A Puppy Named Lady

Others

Invisible Mind

Extradition (coming soon)

Pumpkin Chocolate Chip bread

Sift together: 3 ½ c flour

1 tsp baking powder

2 tsp baking soda

1 tsp salt

½ tsp ground cloves

1 tsp cinnamon

1 tsp nutmeg

1 tsp allspice

Then add:

ACKNOWLEDGMENTS

I wouldn't be able to get anywhere on my books without the continued support of my husband, my family, and the Cookeville writers' group. I appreciate all their hard work in pushing and inspiring me onward.

PROLOGUE

July 1875

Soot blew in the window leaving a trail of dust in its wake. The heat was only enhanced by the suffocating dust flying everywhere. The constant clatter of the train coupled with the heat and soot had put the tall, dark haired man in a foul mood.

Business had been bad lately. It seemed nobody had any money to spare. He sat there trying to figure out another good plan before he had to face his cohorts again. He couldn't go back without any ideas, what kind of leader was he if he couldn't be the brains of the outfit.

The train slowed to a stop. The man sat staring blankly out the window brooding over his turn of luck. A bag bumped him. His head whipped around to curse the careless passenger boarding the train, but what he saw made the words stick in his mouth.

"Excuse me." The clipped words came from the offender who was neatly dressed and well groomed.

The man in the seat smiled at him. "No harm done."

The shoulders of the man standing holding his bag drooped as he realized the last empty seat had been taken.

"Pull ya up a seat." The man in the seat addressed the other. The standing man's dark eyes glanced down, grimaced slightly at the sight of the dusty traveler, and after a moment's hesitation gave in to the invitation.

"What brings ya here?" The dusty traveler asked friendly like.

The well groomed man finally turned in his seat facing his benefactor, and after a slight curl of his nose answered. "I'm on my way to Fort Smith to see about joining business ventures."

"Ah, a business man. I thought so. I jus' so happen to be a business man myself. What sort of business you in?"

"The textile industry. Did you know that ladies fashion is in the middle of a huge revolution? Women everywhere are demanding all the new styles and colors. I'm hoping to see if my uncle can help me open a market in Fort Smith. It seems to be the last civilized place before heading west, and from what I hear the women there need a huge change."

"That sounds promisin'. I've been workin' in this area a while and I'm sure the women would appreciate a change of clothin'."

"It's more than a change of clothing. It's the dawn of a new era!" The well groomed man became more animated as he spoke. He acted like he alone would be the cause of this marvelous revolution.

"Maybe I could help you. I'm in the transportation business mostly, but have been known to expand into other areas. I know the area pretty well too, the land, the people."

The dark eyes of the well dressed man shot to his companion in the slightest bit of doubt.

"Well I don't know. My uncle has been living down here for a number of years. He says he's well connected and should be able to get me started easily enough."

"Tell ya what. If you find you need a little more insight or help, jus' look me up. By the way name's William Whitaker, but most folks call me Whitey."

"Jess, Jess Whitley." The men shook hands.

Whitey couldn't believe his luck. The man in the seat next to him still hadn't seen the resemblance that the two of them shared. If Whitey cut his hair a little and shaved they could almost pass for twins. The idea that had nagged him since Jess sat down began to grow. He needed to court this man's friendship until the opportune time arrived. With a smile still on his face Whitey began asking Jess about his family in Fort Smith, every detail, every life event. Jess loved to talk and it took very little prodding to get what he needed.

The screeching of wheels, the hissing of steam, and a final lurch of the train signaled it was finally time to disembark.

"Let me help you find your way across the river. The ferry is usually crowded and it takes so long. I have connections that will get you across much faster." Whitey offered after the two exited the train and stood on the platform amongst the sea of travelers.

"Could you?"

"Of course. Let me show you firsthand how well connected I am, jus' in case you ever change your mind."

The two men made their way out of the depot and after renting a couple of horses, they made their way out of town. Jess appeared ill at ease on the back of the horse. Whitey smiled. This was the best plan he'd had in months.

An hour later Whitey pulled up reigns. "We need to stop and water the horses."

"So soon? Can't we wait till we get to the river? Surely it can't be that far from here."

"It's the heat. If you make them go too long they'll die midstride. You want to get there right?"

Jess looked around at their surroundings. It was secluded and ominous. He shrugged not seeing an alternative. Truthfully, he was glad for chance to get off the horse. He hadn't ridden in years.

A small creek trickled behind a dense area of woods. Whitey and Jess led their eager horses to the refreshing liquid. Jess bent down to splash some water on his face to cool off when he suddenly felt hands around his throat. The horses shied away from the thrashing that only lasted a minute. The hands around the throat of the limp body kept up the pressure for another minute before being satisfied there was no life left.

Steadily and methodically, Whitey stripped Jess of his clothes and dusted them off from his last struggle. He carefully tucked them into the ridiculous bag Jess had carried, taking care to keep Jess's shoes from dirtying the clothes any more.

Leaving the man only in his under clothes, Whitey turned the two horses back toward the depot. The first thing he needed to do when he reached Fort Smith was get a haircut and shave.

CHAPTER 1

May 1, 1876

A shot pierced the warm night air. The whole universe became silent as it watched the death scene play out in the woods below.

A shocked expression, full of disbelief and sudden fear, creased his face as he peered down at the hole in his stomach with his life blood bubbling out. For a split second, she met his cold brown eyes in one final act of defiance before he collapsed on the earth beneath him, his last breaths fighting to keep from parting with his soul.

A familiar voice spoke to her from the darkness as she lowered her gun. She didn't jump at the sound, she was past feeling. Nothing mattered any more. She was free, free from her burden. It didn't matter what she did now, her oppressor was dead.

The voice in the darkness continued to speak. "Drop it."

Katy let the heavy pistol drop out of her small hands to the ground. She had no more use for it. It had served its purpose. Blood trickled from Jess's mouth now. His eyes were glazed. He wouldn't survive more than another minute or two. Too bad she thought. He should've suffered more for what he'd done.

"Now put your hands in the air." The voice once again demanded.

Lifting her hands, she felt as if she were lifting her hands in rejoicing rather than in punishment. Looking up from under the brim of her hat she met the hard blue eyes of the only person she trusted to rescue her.

"Katy?" Disbelief and shock spread across his face. The pistol aimed at her faltered then lowered completely. "What..?" He started to speak, but the words didn't seem to be able to find their way out.

"Yes it's me, Rex. I'm free now." Confusion and a thousand questions played across her brother's handsome face as he stood there stunned into silence. She couldn't remember a time she'd been so happy to see her older brother. She felt the beginnings of a smile spread across her face. It was a strange feeling. It'd been so long since she'd smiled.

Lowering her raised arms, she practically flew into her big brother.

"What in tarnation!" He grunted as he caught her.

"It's over now. I can go home. Take me home with you, please." She implored him, her arms still holding on to him as if he'd vanish if she let go. Tears began to pool like crystals in her eyes.

Rex looked down at her from the shadows covering his face. "It's not that simple." His voice seemed strained now.

Silence filled the night again. She understood, really she did. He was a U.S. Deputy Marshal now. He had to uphold the law no matter who broke it or for what reason. She would go with him willingly and without a fight. Jail would be nothing compared to what had happened to her since she'd left home.

"I understand Rex, but before you take me in would you listen to what I have to say? Then I'll go with you. You don't have to use your irons and chains on me. I won't run. I want you to hear it first."

Rex lifted his calloused hands to her shoulders and looked into those familiar eyes that were so much like his own. What had become of his little sister? The little girl who would always find injured animals and bring them to their ma to patch up. Then when one of those rescued creatures died, there would be buckets of tears. Sensitive and sweet, that's the Katy he remembered. The small woman who stood before him now, looking confident and relieved, after having just murdered a man in cold blood couldn't be the same sweet, gentle Katy. Granted he'd wanted to kill Jess himself at one time, but to see his own sister do it was almost more than he could take. He'd fought rattlers, rustlers, and a host of other criminals, but he had never had to come face to face with his own blood kin on the other side of the law.

The pair walked past Jess. Rex stopped and checked him. The man was finally dead. He couldn't say he was sorry, he just wished it'd been done a different way. He was afraid of what Katy would tell him. He didn't want to imagine what had driven her to this point. But, she was his sister first of all and he needed to listen to her story. He inhaled deeply, trying to steel his nerves against what was to come.

They seated themselves cross-legged next to each other on the hard packed earth near the fire, Jess's body all but forgotten behind them. The smell of blood and death began to creep into the air. It wouldn't be long until the coyotes would start their death songs and come to investigate. Katy became more relaxed the longer they sat there in silence as she gathered her scattered thoughts. How could she explain the horrors she'd endured to her favorite brother? Should she tell him *everything*, or were there parts that only she needed to know?

Taking a final, resolved breath she spoke.

CHAPTER 2

"You know how hard life was after Pa came back from the war wounded like he was." Katy glanced at Rex looking for some hint of remembrance. A pained expression crossed his face, but vanished just as quickly.

"You 'member how hard we all worked just to eat? After you left it got worse." Looking down at the bare earth again, her vivid mind started playing out scenes that threatened to tumble out of her mouth. "Pa's health declined and I had to take over nearly everythin'. Every girl starts to think of romance and begins to dream when they get to a certain age, but I had no future, no dreams, no hope. I couldn't do what other girls did because we didn't have anythin'. We barely had enough to survive. Ma was so strict with me and Pa's health was so bad I had no one to escort me to socials, even if they'd have let me go. It was nothin' but torture. I lived out my dreams and adventures through the eyes of Sally Mae and the stories she told me…"

August 16, 1873

"Dark clouds rolled in as he spoke. The wind picked up. When he was finally finished saying his last words the trap doors snapped open and he dropped. Lightning struck just as the trap door released! Some woman, I think it was a black woman standing near the wall, screamed *John Childers soul has gone to hell, I heard the chains a clangin'*. The dark skies opened up and drenched all of us! Oh Katy, I so wish you could have been there with me. It was so thrilling!" Sally Mae's voice was exuberant as she recounted her version of the hanging the day before to her best friend Katy.

Sixteen year old Katy stood in front of Sally Mae, hands clasp together and pressed against her heart. Her blue eyes were glowing with excitement.

"Oh Sally Mae, I wish I could've been there too! But Ma says it ain't proper for a young lady my age to go to such gruesome displays. Was Jack Carson there?"

Sally Mae's dark bonneted head nodded exaggeratedly. "He was. I think he had a good view from the hill he stood on."

"He's so handsome! How did he react to it all?" Katy placed her work calloused hands on her friends delicate arm, begging for more information.

"I don't honestly know. I was so enraptured in the moment I didn't think to look." Katy's face fell for only a brief moment. It wasn't fair that Ma wouldn't let her do things other girls did. Sally Mae was barely a year older than she, and her parents let her do all kinds of things like dances, and socials that she was not allowed to attend.

Times like these she wanted to blame her brothers for not being there, James for dying in the war, Sam and Rex for running out on the family, especially Rex after he'd been practically the only brother that she remembered very well. He knew how to talk Ma and Pa into nearly anything. Now that Pa's health was failing he didn't have much energy for anything. He couldn't escort her to any of the social events after a long day on their farm. He was simply too weak. And they were poor. Her current light yellow dress was practically white from wear and was nearly see through. They had no money to buy new fabric to make a new one. She had her Sunday dress and that was all. Ma's dresses were every bit as worn and tattered. She envied Sally Mae's beautiful dresses. She had at least a dozen different ones, and since they were close to the same size she'd even offered to let Katy borrow one if she were ever allowed to a social affair.

But she wasn't. She was practically locked on the little farm her pa owned. She glanced at Sally Mae's dark green dress that was the latest style and accentuated her figure perfectly. She had gentlemen caller's frequently. The only boy who looked at Katy was Kurt Blakely who was so gangly and dopey he made a donkey look like a thoroughbred. Katy inwardly twinged. At the rate things were going that would be her only option at marriage, otherwise she was looking at life as a spinster.

Katy signed again in frustration. One day, one day she'd leave this farm and not have to kill herself to be able to eat all winter.

"What's wrong Katy? You look distraught." Sally Mae asked as she noticed Katy's expression had turned from a joyous revelation to a distant, longing look.

"Oh jus' day dreamin' I suppose. Wishin' I could get off this farm and have the freedom that you do."

Sally Mae's eyes clouded. "Don't think that Katy because some days I wish I could be like you. Your parents actually care about you. Mine are always too busy with this and that. Not to mention that people around here still haven't accepted us fully since we moved here a few years ago. They still give us barely concealed, menacing looks. Like Trace Humphrey over at the livery stable, I wouldn't trust him with our horses. He refuses to even shoe our horses. Father says it's because he fought for the Confederacy. I think he's just plain mean. There are others too, but he's the worst and most open about it."

"Well it sure doesn't do anything to slow down your stream of male followers. I think half the town wants to marry you." Katy said almost pouting.

"Most of them are just after Father's money and they're so boring. There's no reason you should be envious of me. I bet if you were just a little bit cleaned up and had the right clothes, you'd have just as many boys after you as I do."

Katy rolled her eyes at the slight barb to her cleanliness and clothes. Sally Mae knew better than anybody none of that was likely to change in the near future.

Their conversation had just turned to the newest style dresses and what colors they'd each look good in, when Katy saw Pa emerge from the barn. He was walking slow and laboriously. Katy stopped talking mid sentence when she saw him, her eyes wrinkled in worry.

"I need to check on Pa." Katy said as she turned away from Sally Mae and jogged the short distance in her bare feet to catch up to him.

"Pa are you feelin' alright?" Pa stopped walking as he looked down at her. He wasn't above average in height, but he still had a few inches on her, especially in her bare feet. His kindly blue eyes looked pained. His face was pale beneath the red blotchiness of exertion. His face was drawn as it often was. Katy had finally stopped wincing at the pain she saw on his face, but it still didn't make it easier.

"I'm fine Katy. Jus'a lil worn out is all. I wasn't able to get Claire unhitched. Can you finish that for me, sweetheart?"

"Sure, Pa. Go lie down for a while." Katy watched his slow progress to the house. She thought it must be his heart again. A few months ago, Ma had finally brought a doctor to the house after Pa had refused to go time and time again. He'd said that Pa's heart was going bad and he needed to take it easy. Only Pa didn't know how to rest. He was the only man at the house and felt like he was the only one who could put food on their table. Katy helped as much as she could, but there were still things that Pa thought should be his job and his job alone.

After Pa's struggling form disappeared into the house, Katy turned to the barn almost forgetting about Sally Mae in her distress.

"I'll see you in church on Sunday, Katy." Sally Mae called to her, as she waved a gloved hand at her. Katy came out of her self-indulgent pity long enough to wave goodbye to one of her only friends. She noticed the clean lines of the gloved hand. Sally Mae's skin was so white and delicate. Hers was rough and tanned from the work she did around the farm. She didn't look much better than a common farm hand she thought bitterly to herself as she walked into the dimly lit barn to finish what Pa had started.

She shouldn't be so hard on Pa. After all, he only had one hand. He'd lost the other in the war. That stupid war that had taken what could've been a good life for her away before she was even old enough to appreciate it. It'd taken her brothers away in more ways than just death. If she could change just one thing it would be to bring her brothers home. Pa's health would improve if they were here to help. She would be allowed to go places and do things that she wasn't now. Their farm might even improve enough to bring in enough money to buy material for another dress. She sighed an exasperated sigh as she unhitched Claire, their poor broken down farm horse that looked just as bad as everything else did.

One day, she promised herself, one day all this would change. She'd find a way to marry a man who had a little money if not lots of it, and then she'd never work again a day in her life. The calluses on her hands would go away. The blisters would be no more. She and Sally Mae could sit on each other's porches, sipping lemonade, and discussing the latest styles and fashions all day.

CHAPTER 3

"I know it couldn't have been easy for you, but they loved you and babied you. You had to have seen that." Rex wanted to add that Sally Mae was nothing more than a pretty face and was about as empty headed as a rock, but he didn't. Sally Mae may be the only one who would accept her, maybe, when she came back to Fort Smith.

"I know they loved me, but love doesn't make the crops grow. I worked next to Pa nearly every day. Then when he got worse I picked up where he left off. I tried so hard to keep them both goin', but Ma's whole life revolved around Pa. My life seemed completely hopeless then. We were destitute." Tears threatened to break from their dam behind her eyes. She didn't think she had any more left. She didn't even realize she could still feel.

Early May 1875

Rain was usually a welcome relief, but the days that followed were nothing short of unbearable sometimes. The damp air was oppressing. Today was one of those times. The oppression wasn't just from the humid air though, Pa was down again. This time he'd been laid up for a few days. Katy's feet trudged sluggishly through the mud from the recent rains. She was tired. Tired of working like she had, tired of Pa being sick, tired of seeing Ma's tears when she thought no one was watching, just tired. Even now in the wee hours of daylight --the air was damp and warm promising a miserable summer to come. Katy wiped a trickle of sweat away from her eye.

Concern for Pa was a heavy burden that slowed her steps and made each chore ten times harder than usual. If Pa died, life on the farm would be sheer torture. Maybe then Ma would be tempted to go live in town with Aunt Stella at her boarding house. She wouldn't have to work like a man every day. Katy found little comfort in the thought. As much as she wanted off their farm, the thought of Pa dying was unbearable, but it might be something she had to face sooner than what she wanted.

"Katy." Ma's soft voice came from behind her as she leaned over the fence daydreaming about a better, happier life. "I need you to go to town today. This letter needs to be mailed immediately. Finish up what you've started and then go."

Katy thought the worry lines in Ma's face had deepened, dark circles hung under her eyes like a ghost. A flittering thought of Ma dying beside Pa threatened to bring unbidden tears to her eyes. She glanced down at the yellowed envelope being handed to her. Rex Redfern was neatly written on one envelope and Sam Redfern on the other. Ma was summoning her remaining sons home. Katy sucked in a breath. Ma must think Pa was near death or she wouldn't be calling her roving sons home. Ma wouldn't meet her eyes. She just stared at the two envelopes as if she could summon them home just by thinking about them hard enough. Katy took the envelopes and hurried away.

After finishing up the rest of her chores, at least the ones that couldn't wait till later, she saddled Claire and started for town. Her heart pounded in her chest. It wasn't the exertion of the chores and the ride so much as what the letters she carried meant. The thoughts of what if's made her dig her heels into Claire as she put her into a fast trot.

By the time the letters were mailed and Katy had turned Claire back toward their home, she had worked herself into such a state that she blinked away tears to clear her blurry vision. She wasn't ready to go home yet, she needed to calm down first. If she didn't, she knew she would breakdown into a blubbery mess on Ma. She had to be the strong one, there was no one else to fill that place. She thought about dropping by to see Aunt Stella, then decided against it. So she turned off the road to Sally Mae's instead.

Sally Mae's house was large and elegant. Just last month she'd come here for a ball. The only reason she'd been invited in the first place was that she was Sally Mae's friend. Pa had raised disapproving eyebrows when she'd asked, but Ma finally had interceded on her behalf. She'd borrowed one of Sally Mae's dresses from last year to wear and for once in her life she felt beautiful and had enjoyed herself as she forgot about all her troubles for a few hours. Katy sighed at the memory. If Pa died there would be no more dances, or anything fun for a long time. Katy dismounted and walked up to the front door.

The echo of her knock sounded loud in the quiet of the afternoon. She was just about to turn and walk around back when the door opened. Sally Mae herself stood in the door way. Her face brightened at the sight of her friend, but fell just as quickly as she noticed the look on Katy's face and her sagging shoulders.

"Come in, Katy. You look like you're carrying the cares of the world on your shoulders. Is your pa down again?" Sally Mae asked gently. For all her money and status, Sally Mae had a kind heart Katy thought as she crossed the threshold into the elaborate foyer. Raising her eyes from the floor, the dam of tears threatened to break at the concerned look Sally Mae was giving her.

"It's not jus' that he's down again. It's that Ma has summoned my brothers. It means that Pa's worse than he's ever been before and Ma's given up on him as dyin' and…" she sniffed trying to hold back the tears, " and I don't know what's goin' to happen to us if he does." The tears she'd fought against so hard finally broke loose and spilled down her cheeks.

She felt herself being guided. Her heavy feet trudged wearily, carrying the weight of her worries and body. She was vaguely aware of sitting down on something soft. Sally Mae handed her a kerchief and sat down next to her.

After a few shoulder shaking minutes of tears, Katy finally started to pull herself together. She sat there glassy-eyed. Sally Mae sat there quietly, patiently waiting for Katy to speak. They were in Sally Mae's quaint room. It was bigger than Katy's little room at home by far. Sally Mae's room alone could hold almost half of their house Katy thought. The window was open, the curtains with the tiny flower patterns fluttered in a rare late spring breeze. The closet was full of colorful dresses. Sally Mae had her own wash stand in her room. Every time she came here she felt a little bit of envy toward her friend. Sally Mae wasn't one to flaunt her status unless she was on a mission, which was usually when she was after a man that was fairly well off himself. Katy took a deep breath and started again.

"Ma sent for my brothers. I don't know if they'll come or not. Pa's really bad this time. This has been the longest he's ever been down. Ma is worn down to the bone. She may die if Pa does." She took another shuddering deep breath at the prospect of becoming an orphan.

"Don't worry Katy, your ma is strong. So is your pa. They'll both be ok and in a few weeks when everyone is feeling better we can go for a picnic or something."

"You really think so?" The voice sounded like a small child asking its mother for reassurance.

"I know so. Now would you like a drink of water or tea?" Katy almost giggled. Sally Mae's parents were impossibly proper in some aspects. Tea was a staple in their house and offered to guests who visited, no matter their status.

"I'd like some water." They both rose from the bed and walked down the stairs to the well outside. The small structure, that resembled a hut, shaded them from the sun's warming rays while they sat near the well and drank water together.

"I know you haven't talked about your brothers much before only to say they were off who knows where. Will you tell me about them?" Sally Mae asked.

Katy looked at her friend for a second as she briefly pondered her motive. Deciding it was just friendly conversation, she began her story.

"It all started when that stupid war broke out. Pa and my oldest brother James went off to fight for the Confederacy." Katy's eyes flashed to Sally Mae for a moment, knowing her kin had fought on the opposite side.

"It's ok Katy. The war's over. We won't let it stand in the way of our friendship." Sally Mae smiled reassuringly. Katy faintly nodded.

"So that left Sam and Rex at home. Sam was sixteen and they said Ma pleaded with him not to go, but he ran off and went anyway. I don't remember much of that because I was so young. I jus' remember being scared all the time. Rex was the one who was left, and he was only twelve. Ma said he did a man's work on the farm we had in Dover. When the war was over, James was dead. Pa was the way he is now, only not so sick." She knew Sally Mae had seen her Pa's missing left hand. "Sam came home, but he was different than I remembered him. Two years does a lot to a child's memory and as I got older I wondered 'bout it a lot. He was quiet and sullen. He left home again within two years after the war. Rex had practically been the man around the house since the war. But then he turned eighteen and he took off shortly after. He's come home for a visit once or twice since then, but that's 'bout it. I was still young, but I could tell he was restless. Somethin' drove him away and I didn't know what. I'm startin' to think it was the family responsibility. He always was gettin' into trouble in his free time. Ma thinks he's workin' as a guard on the Missouri, Kansas, Texas railroad. It wouldn't surprise me if Ma's letter found him locked up in jail somewhere for robbin' the train!"

The tinkling laugh Katy elicited from her friend made her smile. "Surely you don't mean that!"

"I'm not so sure I don't." They were both still smiling. Katy sobered. "I jus' hope he makes it back in time, or at least comes back."

"Me too Katy, me too." Sally Mae gave Katy a short hug.

Katy let out an exasperated sigh. "Well I better get back home. I still have work to do."

"Alright. I'll come see you in a few days."

"I'd like that. Thanks Sally Mae. Sorry I fell apart like that on you."

"Don't worry about it." They parted ways and Katy turned Claire back toward their little farm, hoping Sally Mae was right and at least one of her brothers would make it home before Pa died.

Almost two weeks had passed since her visit with Sally Mae and with still no word from her brothers. Katy knew the mail travelled slow, but they could at least send a telegram. Maybe she would ask Ma to go to town later and check with the telegraph office and see if they had.

For the last three days she had found Pa out in the barn or out in the fields when she was doing her daily chores. It made her worry about him even more. He insisted he was fine and needed to get back to work. But every night he came in and he looked like he was barely breathing. Katy would find him resting often. She tried to convince him repeatedly that she was perfectly capable to handle things, but he waved her off and told her it wasn't a woman's place, that she should be helping Ma. She ignored him and tried to get the work done before he could get to it.

The sun was hotter today than it had been so far this spring. It felt as if summer was already in full swing. Katy was in the barn when Ma poked her head in.

"Is your pa in here?" Ma had a plate of food and a pail of water.

"No I think he's out in the field somewhere." Ma frowned. Katy knew how she felt. She argued vehemently with Pa that morning over going into the field. That was part of the reason she was in the barn now is because she couldn't bear to watch him struggle and push himself beyond his limits.

Ma turned and left. Katy turned back to her work.

A few minutes later Katy heard the most eerie, nerve wracking sound she'd ever heard. Her stomach fell. She knew something was bad wrong. She ran out of the barn, searching in vain for the source of the sound.

At first she didn't see it. Then she saw it. A movement to her right. She looked closer. It looked like Ma was bent over. Had she been hurt? Katy's bare feet flew over the ground and out into the field where Ma was barely visible over the green shoots.

Ma was bent over something. Katy stopped dead in her tracks as she realized what it was. Pa lay on the ground and it didn't look like he was moving. Ma was shaking uncontrollably. Katy felt paralyzed. She knew what was wrong without asking. She was moving forward without a conscious thought. She placed a hand on Ma's back before she knew what she was doing. The tears didn't come at first. They were too shocked to flow.

Whether it had been minutes or hours or even days, Katy didn't know. She looked up from where she knelt near Ma's quiet form still bent over Pa's body. There were no brothers to come rescue them. There were no hands to call for help to move Pa's body. There were no arms of comfort to fall into. There was nothing. Her dull eyes roved over their small plot of land as silent tears slid down her cheeks. Her life was no longer in her control. She was tied to this place. Tied to helping Ma. Tied to trying to live one day to the next. She felt deserted, abandoned, and more alone than she ever had in her life. Marriage was nothing more than a fancy word that other girls got to talk about. Happiness was a word than meant nothing. The sun was bright in the sky, but Katy only saw dark clouds on the horizon.

CHAPTER 4

Through blurred vision Katy looked over at Rex. She thought she saw tears glistening in his eyes, but shadows often played tricks. She released a shuddering breath she hadn't realized she still held. Her voice came out stronger than she felt.

"When you came home I thought life would go back to some semblance of normality. After your first encounter with Sally Mae I had it all figured out."

The next few days were a blur. Somehow they'd come to own a black dress. Normally Katy would be ecstatic about another dress, but black was not her color. She hated it. Ma insisted that it was the proper thing to do so Katy let her arguments rest for her sake. It wasn't like anyone would see them wearing black where they lived anyway. Neighbors visited now while they were in the first stages of mourning, but they would dwindle and pass. Katy felt she'd been dealt a rotten blow by life. She was angry. She was sad. She was a nest of mixed emotions.

Ma was visibly shaken by the whole affair, but after Pa was laid to rest she seemed to grow a strength from somewhere within her. Katy didn't know how she did it. She still felt shaken and insecure. Ma didn't have a whole life time to miss out on, she did.

The third day after Pa's death, Katy saw a lone figure walking toward the house as she walked outside with a basket of soggy laundry. It was probably just another neighbor with empty words of condolence. Then something in the way the man walked made her stop. The voice that spoke her name, it was so familiar. It couldn't be.

"Rex? Is that really you?" She dropped her basket and ran to him. She collapsed into his arms. "Where have you been? How are you? Did you get Ma's letter?" She finally stepped back and looked up at him. He had a surprised but concerned look on his handsome face. He'd aged from a boy to a man since she'd seen him. The flow of questions finally stopped as she took a breath.

"I'm fine. I could've been here a week ago, but had a few mishaps. How's Pa? How's Ma holdin' up?" He paused for a minute. His blue eyes held as many questions for her as she had for him. He was home! That was all that mattered now. Someone had come to help them, to help relieve some of the burden that had been placed on her shoulders.

Finally she knew she could no longer put off the inevitable. She had to tell him. Tears threatened again as she thought about it.

"Pa died three days ago. Ma found him in the field." It was all she could do to spill it all out before she crumbled. The weight of the last few years came tumbling down at last, even after she thought she'd cried her last tear. She fell back into the safe arms of her big brother. He had come to save them.

Before she knew what was happening Ma had joined them in a family hug. They stood there for several silent minutes appreciating the physical nearness of family that cared. Rex felt like the support beam of the family. They would be stable again without so much uncertainty. Her steps were light when they finally made their way back into the house.

Running out the door later that evening, Katy rescued the forgotten basket of laundry and finished hanging it out. Ma was cooking a feast in honor of her son's return home. The food the neighbors had been bringing in the last few days, Ma declared, was unfit for their little celebration.

"You mentioned somethin' 'bout bein' held up by some unfortunate events on your way home. What happened?" Rex had finally stopped eating. The trio had wondered out onto the porch, where the coolness of the evening beckoned. Ma's question seemed to pull him from some distant thought because it took him a minute to answer.

"Well, I got your letter jus' before my last run down to Texas for the KATY railroad. Me and this other feller named Heck were ridin' guard on the express car. We were stoppin' for water at our last water stop before our station and got held up by a gang of outlaws."

"You weren't hurt were you?" Ma gasp as concern clouded her eyes.

"No, we all came out ok." Rex grinned. Katy thought she had a handsome brother. He really was one of the good guys after all. "The robbers didn't though. You shoulda seen it. Heck cut out newspapers that were the same size and shape as paper money and put that in the sack instead of the real money. I'd have loved to seen their faces when they opened that sack of newspapers." He laughed out loud.

It was the first laughter Katy had heard in a long time. An idea began to grow. Sally Mae really should meet him. Sally Mae was so sweet and pretty. Rex was handsome and just as charming as she remembered as a kid. Yes, that's what she would do. It was time for little sister to play matchmaker. Her best friend and favorite brother would be happy and he'd stay here. Life would be close to perfect.

"Anyway we got to Waco and the sheriff there told us to hang around town for a few days while they went and tried to track down the train robbers. I finally convinced them to let me leave and come home. I showed them your letter and he caved in. Took me three days to get outta there. Then when I got off the train in Atoka to catch the stage it took another day and a half for the stage to get there. I didn't think I was ever gonna make it."

"Well you're here now and that's all that matters. I'm jus' glad you made it safely." Katy watched a fleeting shadow of doubt cross Rex's face. She recognized the look as the same one he had on his face when he told her he was leaving home. She didn't like that look at all. She needed to get Sally Mae to visit soon so he'd have something to stay here for, otherwise she was afraid he'd take off again. She couldn't let him, not when her life was so close to being perfect.

The conversation took a more sobering turn as Ma and Rex started talking about Pa and what had caused his decline and eventual death. Katy couldn't bear it anymore and left the porch to go to what she liked to call her thinking spot. A small creek ran along the far back side of their land, and along the banks there was a deeper cut out place with somewhat of a plateau before the water's edge. A neat stand of trees shielded the cove from the average eye. She'd found it several years ago and had come back when things got tough. When the weather was warm enough she'd sit and put her feet and legs in or wade out in the cool running water. All this she usually did during the daylight hours. She never came after dark. Lately it'd been because she'd been too tired, but she also knew during the warmer season that snakes and other night creature may find her spot just as comfortable as she did. Tonight she was taking that chance. She just hoped that there were no other inhabitants to keep her company.

Two weeks had passed since Rex's return home and Katy still hadn't had an opportunity to visit Sally Mae. She was half surprised Sally Mae hadn't stopped by to see her, but then she was probably being wooed by some man again and comfortably preoccupied. She sat down next to the second of their two dairy cows and started milking. Her mind was miles away. Rex had left to venture into town for some reason or another. She didn't really care what it was. She was too busy trying to figure out how to get Sally Mae to meet her brother.

The day was half over when her dilemma solved itself. A horse drawn buggy appeared in the drive. It was none other than Sally Mae herself. Katy rushed into the house to wash her hands and face before her friend could see how dirty she looked today. She walked back outside just as Sally Mae called a halt to her horse and got out.

"Sally Mae! I'm so glad you came."

"I've been trying to get over here for days, but Mother has me helping her with some social that we're having at our house in a few days." Sally Mae waved her delicate hand dismissively. For a fleeting instant Katy thought about trying to get herself invited to the social, but in the end decided against it. She still didn't have a nice dress to wear. It would look bad if she borrowed another one of Sally Mae's, not to mention it would be considered improper to appear out of mourning so soon.

"That's ok. My brother, Rex, came home about two weeks ago. He's been here helpin' us so it hasn't been as bad."

Sally Mae's eyes flitted around for a brief second in search of the mysterious brother. Katy smiled to herself. That was a good sign, interest. "Oh that's good to hear. How's your ma holding up?"

"She's been doin' really good actually. I think a lot of it has to do with Rex comin' home though. I jus' hope he stays for a while. I'm not so sure he will. Whenever Ma asks him, he avoids a direct answer." Sally Mae frowned.

"Do you think he'll leave again?"

"Maybe. I don't know." The happiness she'd felt at seeing her friend dimmed at the thought of Rex leaving them alone again.

"Never mind about that, let me tell you about what Mother is doing now." Sally Mae took her by the arm and they walked part of the outer edges of the farm in the shade of the bordering tree line.

By the time they made it back to the well for a drink of water, Katy was laughing again. She'd temporarily forgotten her fears of Rex leaving again. Sally Mae had successfully made her mood lighten.

"Have you seen Tom Hardy lately?" Tom was Katy's latest fascination. He was barely over twenty years old. His family had a decent sized farm not far down the road, and they were known to make occasional appearances at the church both girls attended.

"Haven't seen him in a while, but they're probably busy with their crops and such." Sally Mae waved dismissively.

They stood near the well sharing lighthearted conversation, when she saw Rex, unexpectedly, come out of the barn. She hadn't heard or seen him come in and it surprised her. He started for the house then seemed to freeze in his tracks. He looked at Sally Mae like he'd seen a ghost. The expression cleared before Katy could read it.

"Rex," she called to him. "Come meet my friend."

He didn't look happy as he approached. She hoped it was from something that'd happened in town and not his reaction to Sally Mae.

"Sally Mae this is my brother Rex. Rex this is my friend Sally Mae. We didn't hear you come up. When did you get back?"

"Not long ago. I had to come back early to get ready for tomorrow." Katy wished he would smile. He wore a sour expression on his face that didn't bode well for her plans.

"What's happenin' tomorrow that's so important?" If he'd already found another woman she wanted to know it now before she pushed Sally Mae into his arms.

"I'm ridin' out at first light with Deputy Marshal Spencer. Goin' lookin' for some decayin' bones. Nice to meet you Sally Mae, but I need to go see Ma and I'm short on time." He tipped his hat before either of them could say another word and left.

Katy turned to her friend. "I'm sorry. I don't know what's come over him today. He's usually more friendly and not quite so rude."

"Don't worry about it. He's probably worried about you and your ma." Sally Mae spoke but her eyes never left Rex's retreating form.

Katy smiled to herself. Usually once Sally Mae set her sights on something she didn't give up until she got it, and right now Katy's brother was in her sights. Katy didn't think she knew much about a lot of things, but she did know her friend.

They talked a few minutes longer before Sally Mae declared she had to go home. She waved goodbye and Katy watched her retreating form for a few moments before she turned back to see if she could help Ma with supper, and maybe say a few good words to Rex about Sally Mae.

CHAPTER 5

"I knew you were happy I was home. I tried to be a good brother and son, but I'd been gone too long. I'm not a farmer. I can't settle down. If I ever settle down it'll probably eat me alive. This is my life now." Rex flipped open his vest revealing his shiny tin star. "This land needs law and swift justice brought to it if it's goin' to flourish. I know you and Ma needed me and I tried to be there when I could, but I also knew ya'll could make it without me. Here," he motioned his hand around them, "they have no protectors. I tried once to explain it to Sally Mae, but she didn't understand. You may not either."

"I understand a lot more now than I did. I can understand why you left the farm. I can understand that you want to help others, but you weren't there when I needed you most. I was weak and naïve. I fell for a few pretty words and a handsome face.

That's what you have to understand. I was still just a kid inside."

Everything was a blur the next couple weeks to Katy. Life went back to being just what it had been before Rex came home. He was gone again and she was stuck there. Stuck doing the work of three men, ok, so maybe two, but doing a man's work never the less. In a way she understood her brother's restlessness and on the other hand she envied him that he had the means and opportunity. Unlike herself who was stuck, stuck, stuck. She stabbed at the hay with the pitchfork as if by doing so it would take away her anger and frustration.

The heat and her temper made Katy miserable all day. She was debating alternative ways of getting away from home when a familiar figure came riding up. It was Rex. Katy let out somewhat of a relieved sigh and sat down where she was. Help had arrived. She didn't run to him like she had when he first came home. She was still miffed at him for leaving and she suspected this was only the beginning.

It was time to call it a day. She didn't care that she hadn't finished what she'd started that day. She was bone weary and tired. Rex could help her with it tomorrow. She stood from her position on the ground and went to put her tools up in the barn. Ma would be happy to have Rex home again. At least something good turned out of it.

"Hi Katy, I'm home." Katy turned to Rex who'd come into the barn a minute after she had.

"Obviously." She turned back around, not caring that his expression changed from relief to concern at the venom of her words.

"What's wrong Katy? Why're ya mad at me?" He put his new horse, Blaze, in his stall then walked up to her when she hadn't responded yet.

"Nothin'." She muttered under her breath. He wouldn't understand anyway.

"C'mon. I know you better than that. You're lyin' through yer teeth. Tell me what's wrong and why yer mad at me." He gently turned her to face him.

Somewhere she dug up the courage to meet his eyes. "I…" she stopped as she caught sight of something strange on his hat. "What on earth is on yer head?"

"Huh? Oh." He removed his hat to let her take a closer look at it. "That trip I went on was kinda wild. I got lowered into a rattlesnake pit and came out with this."

Katy looked at him incredulously. "Ma is goin' to have a ring-tail fit when she sees that."

He looked temporarily chastised then his charming smile came back. "Don't worry I'll handle Ma." He sobered again. "Now tell me what you were 'bout too, 'bout why you got a chip on yer shoulder."

"You don't give up do you?"

"Nope."

"Well it's jus' that I'm stuck here doin' yer job while you go run all over the country and get to have fun. I'm stuck here workin' like a mule. I have no prospects for a husband and who'd want to marry a woman who works like man and looks like one too? Who? If I was a man I'd have left long time ago too, but because I'm a woman I'm stuck here on this God-forsaken piece of dirt with no future." Angry tears threatened and she turned away. She stalked off to the house without looking back leaving a bewildered Rex.

"Will you hang these clothes out for me Katy? I need to make up some soup for Mrs. Richards down the road." Ma rarely asked her to do her work for her and she became instantly alert.

"Sure Ma. Are ya gonna take it to her when it's done?"

"Yes."

"Can I take it to her please?" Ma looked hesitant. "Please?"

"Oh I suppose it wouldn't hurt. Finish what you can while I get the soup ready."

With a spring in her step, Katy finished hanging the laundry. She did a few other quick chores before she went inside to check on the soup. Rex was out in the field somewhere. She didn't really care where. He could stay there for all she cared. She was free for while today, even if it was to deliver soup to old Mrs. Richards. She was one of their nosiest neighbors, but mostly kind despite it all.

The other good thing about going to see Mrs. Richards was Sally Mae's cutoff was just before her house. On the way home, she might just happen to stop by and pick up Sally Mae. She had to work harder at her match making skills. Rex was still of the mindset that he had to leave.

Mrs. Richards seemed to be on the mend. She was sitting at her kitchen table when Katy arrived. Katy tried to be as cordial as possible, but Mrs. Richards seemed stuck on the subject of Ma and Katy's fate, and Katy's lack of a future. As soon as it was appropriate, Katy made her exit. She was feeling more depressed now than ever, especially after an outsider pointed out what she already knew. She really needed Sally Mae's shoulder.

As Katy drew near the house, she caught a glimpse of a figure dart into the house and unless she missed her guess it was Rex. It seemed a little early for him to be going inside which made Katy's senses tingle with suspicion. They walked into the house after putting Claire in the barn. Katy called out to Ma.

"Mrs. Richards said to tell you thank you for the soup. Sally Mae was visitin' her too and came home with me." The two of them stopped at the kitchen door. Rex was standing in the kitchen with Ma, which was unusual and Katy instantly knew by the look on Ma's face that he was leaving again.

"Hi Sally Mae, how's your folks?" Ma asked looking somewhat relieved at the sight of them.

"They're fine Mrs. Redfern. Thanks for asking." Katy barely heard the exchange. She'd been watching Rex's reaction closely. He didn't look impressed. In fact, he looked annoyed. Katy needed a plan, she thought, as he made a hasty exit.

"Will you be stayin' for supper?" Ma asked Sally Mae.

"Oh please, Sally Mae. I'll take you home later." Katy chimed in. She watched as Sally Mae flashed a quick look at the doorway Rex had just vacated and smiled. Yes, this would work out perfectly.

"I suppose I could."

"Good." Katy was satisfied.

"Can I help with anything?" Sally Mae offered.

"Well," Ma paused for a minute thinking. "As a matter of fact, how are you at makin' biscuits?"

"I can handle them."

"Good. Rex jus' came in askin' for biscuits to take with him. He's leavin' out again tomorrow. I'll let you handle that while Katy helps me finish the rest of supper."

Evening shadows were growing longer and darker as the sun dipped slowly on the western horizon. Katy was day dreaming about her best friend becoming her sister in law when Rex finally showed his face for dinner. He carried one of Sally Mae's biscuits in one hand that he'd picked up in the kitchen on his way in.

"Thanks Ma. I'll have a hard time keepin' these biscuit to myself." Rex said chewing a bite of biscuit appreciatively.

"Actually, Sally Mae made them. You can thank her." Ma said politely giving the appropriate credit. Katy almost burst out laughing at the look on Rex's face. He looked like he'd swallowed a frog when Ma told him who'd made the biscuits. Sally Mae kept silent, for once playing the part of the subdued, proper woman. Katy was silently cheering. Ma's unknowing help and Sally Mae being Sally Mae, her plan just might work after all.

Dinner turned out to be one of the most lighthearted and happiest Katy could remember. Ma smiled often, Rex even cracked a grin, and Katy herself felt laughter bubble out at some of Rex's stories.

"Mrs. Redfern, thank you for dinner. It's been wonderful, but I'm afraid I need to be leaving." Sally Mae finally said.

Katy was about to get up and get Clair hitched to the wagon when Rex jumped in and offered to take her home. Katy and Ma exchanged glances. This was unusual for Rex, considering his rudeness toward her nearly every other time they'd met. Ma must've thought the same thing. Katy might have to talk to her and they could plot together. Surely they could figure out how to get Rex to fall for Sally Mae. Ma liked Sally Mae too, so it wasn't a matter of approval.

Katy's hopes only briefly fell when Rex didn't linger in taking Sally Mae home. He was back faster that she herself would've been. He also seemed to be brooding slightly more than usual. She couldn't figure out why he was so stand offish with Sally Mae when he was so charming with most everyone else, especially the women. She sighed, threw up her hands in exasperation, before she went to their shared room to sleep. She wasn't getting her wish tonight so there was no point in staying up hoping.

Katy sat in the shade of Sally Mae's covered porch tapping her foot rapidly in frustration. She'd convinced Ma that if she didn't have a break from the work at home she was going to collapse from exhaustion. It was true, partially. Since Pa's death she'd pulled the weight of any man and she hadn't been quite half the size of Pa who was the smallest man in their family. Ma helped out of the house some, but if they were to eat, one of them had to take care of the meals. That left Katy with the back breaking work. Her youthfulness gave her the energy she needed, but it also filled her with restlessness.

"I'm tellin' you Sally Mae I don't know what I'm gonna do. I can't take it anymore. If I could jus' find a decent man to marry, I could survive till I'm twenty at least. At this rate I'll be dead before my next birthday."

Sally Mae clicked her tongue and shook her head in dismay.

"What about the Marque's boy, what's his name?"

"Kevin." Katy said disgustedly. "He's interested in Hattie, least wise that what the talk at church is."

Sally Mae nodded as if that made sense to her.

"I hate my life. I hate the dirt. I hate the fields..." Katy was about to continue on her list of all the things she hated, but the approach of a lone rider stopped her tirade. Both women stilled as they observed the approaching horseman. Katy wanted to moan. It was probably one of Sally Mae's suitors. For once, why couldn't she have someone call on her?

The man stopped short before the porch.

"Is this the Gibbons house?" His voice was smooth and rich. His speech sounded cultured. Katy glanced at Sally Mae. Was this one of her suitors? Sally Mae's expression was just as startled as her own must be.

"Yes it is. Are you looking for my father?" The man dismounted and walked up the three steps to the women on the porch who stood to greet him.

"Allow me to introduce myself. I'm Jess Whitley. I'm your cousin. Your father is my uncle on my mother's side." He took each woman's proffered hand, and as he held it he bowed his head to each of them.

"It's a pleasure to meet you. I've heard about you. I believe you sent Father a letter back in the spring about your possible arrival."

"Yes I did. I was so happy to hear he'd accept me into his house for a short spell."

"Please come in. Let me fetch Father." Sally Mae led the two visitors into the house.

Katy could barely help herself. Her eyes kept straying to the tall man with the dark hair and eyes. He had a smile that could melt butter. He glanced at her as they took a seat in the parlor to wait for Sally Mae to fetch her father.

"Are you a friend of the family?" Jess asked.

"I'm Sally Mae's friend Katy." He held her eyes. She almost forgot to breath he was so handsome.

"It's a pleasure to meet you." She couldn't think of a reply. Her brain was mush.

Footsteps in the hall saved her from any more embarrassment when Sally Mae and her father entered the room.

"I have to go." Katy whispered to Sally Mae as she headed for the door. She'd looked down at her dress a moment before and suddenly became very self conscience. She appeared to be an orphan. Her dress was patched in so many places it looked like it was made of Swiss cheese. Her finger nails were filthy and rugged. The only femininity she possessed was lost under the veil of her rugged appearance.

"Would you and your ma like to join us for dinner tomorrow?" Sally Mae asked. Katy brought her eyes up from the floor to make sure she wasn't making an empty gesture. Sally Mae looked sincere.

"I'll ask to make sure, but I don't see a problem with it."

"Fantastic. I'll see you tomorrow then Katy." Sally Mae said enthusiastically.

"See you then." As the shock wore off, she mentally scolded herself for acting like such a tongue-tied school girl as she rushed from the room, and practically ran out the front door.

"Ma! Ma! Sally Mae jus' asked us to come to dinner tomorrow. We can go right?" Katy was almost breathless with excitement by the time she reached the house.

"I suppose it couldn't hurt. You've been workin' awfully hard lately." Ma's gaze was full of pride, and maybe a little sadness, she wasn't certain.

Squealing like a child, Katy gave Ma a quick hug. Deciding to get a head start on the next day's chores, she went out to start her work early. It helped that she had something to distract her thoughts, a tall, dark, handsome man. As she worked, she would close her eyes and think about was the way that Jess had looked at her. She'd felt so dirty and ugly, yet she hadn't seen a trace of repulsion on his face. She let her imagination roam. It was like a ray of sunshine after a terrible storm.

CHAPTER 6

"For the first time in my life I was beginnin' to feel like a woman and not like a work horse. Jess said all the right things and he seemed the only way out. What else could I ask for?"

Sitting quietly and unmoving, Rex let her go on uninterrupted. He sensed this was hard for her to accept that she'd been so gullible and naïve. The bitterness in her voice told him more than her words.

"I was blind and desperate. I knew what he was before I left. I also knew what you and Ma would say if you were to ever find out, but that didn't matter. It was the end of my life as a slave to the land. It was an escape, a free passage to my dreams." A cold and hollow look came back into her eyes. Rex hated to see it. He'd seen it in too many men, murders and rapist, who no longer cared what happened to others. He wanted to shake the look from his sister's eyes and tell there was hope, there was a future. However, he didn't know what that future held.

In her Sunday dress, face scrubbed, hair brushed and somewhat styled, Katy felt like royalty dining at the ornately carved table with matching chairs. The food had been nothing short of perfect. In fact the whole evening had been perfect.

At first Katy had been apprehensive about meeting Jess again, but he had a carefree manner that seemed to light up the room. Even Ma, who was usually quiet, had joined in the conversations.

Across from Katy was Jess, in his carefully pressed clothes and butter melting smile. She'd watched him watching her half the evening. She'd planned to eat very little and appear to be a proper lady, but the food had been so delicious that now she sat there feeling like a fat pig just before butchering.

"Katy, would you like to take a walk with me outside. The moon should be full tonight." Jess asked as the dinner party began to dismiss to the parlor. Forgetting her questionable ability to walk after eating so much, she agreed.

His arm was warm and strong as she took it. She'd never been for a walk by the light of the moon before. He was tall like Rex only broader. His confidence emanated from every part of him. For a fleeting moment she feared what Ma would say when she found out, but quickly dismissed it in lieu of spending time in this handsome man's company.

They walked for several minutes speaking meaningless things. Katy was beginning to wonder if he was just passing time while he was here and just being nice out of courtesy to his cousin.

"Sally Mae tells me you and your ma are all alone out on your farm." Katy stiffened slightly. She wasn't sure how to take his probing into her life. She looked up at him. His face was warm and gentle. He didn't seem like he was asking out of malice.

"Pretty much. Pa died couple months ago. I have a brother that comes in some and helps a lil bit here and there, but," she shrugged, "it's mainly jus' the two of us."

"That's a shame. A pretty girl like you shouldn't have to be doing a man's work. You should have a man working for you."

"Unfortunately, there's not many options when you're in my shoes." As soon as the words left her mouth she wished she could grab them and put them back. She may not be properly educated in the ways of courtship, but she knew it was improper to speak of one's misfortunes. Jess didn't seem to notice.

"You only need one good one though." He smiled at her then and she wondered if he wanted to be that one for her. It made her senses tingle when she thought about it. They had almost made their way around the house.

Silence engulfed them for several steps before he spoke again. "Would you mind if I called on you while I'm in town?"

Stunned speechless, Katy stopped in her tracks. "Please don't take offense. It's just that I don't know anyone in town and being stuck here in this house... well sometimes it can get kind of stuffy."

"Sure. I'm sure that'll be fine." Katy finally managed to find her voice to answer.

On the way home a short time later, Katy thought she would burst. She was filled with excited energy. One of the most handsome men she'd ever met was going to call on her. She knew she wouldn't sleep tonight. Ma quietly endured her excited babble and cautioned her against friendly men and the dangers they presented. Katy barely heard, all she could do was dream about Jess and the sliver of hope it presented for her.

However, when almost a week had passed with no sign of Jess, Katy's hopes began to wane. Maybe he'd just been making polite conversation. Maybe he found someone else who was more feminine. Maybe, maybe, maybe, the doubt assailed her. She was on the verge of breaking down in despair and crying into the dirt when a familiar buggy appeared. She forced herself not to run to him like a child in anticipation.

"Hello Jess."

"Hello Katy. How're you today?" She felt nervous again. She started wiping her dirty hands on the back of her dress.

"I'm fine."

"Could you get away for a little while and go for a picnic with me?"

"Now?"

"Now." He smiled his beguiling smile at her and she had no will power to say no. Rex was still gone, but she could put off work for one afternoon.

"Sure. Let me tell Ma so she doesn't worry." She turned and ran into the house. She didn't really give Ma a chance to respond before she ran back out again. When she realized she was running, she slowed to a walk so she wouldn't appear so unladylike. She climbed into the seat next to Jess and he flicked the reigns.

"Do you know any places where we could picnic?" Jess asked her.

"We could go down near the river."

"The river it is." Jess turned the buggy and headed toward town and the Arkansas River.

Stepping lightly and humming to herself, Katy felt some of the oppressive burden that had been placed on her shoulders lifted as she set about her work on the farm. The picnic with Jess had been nothing short of perfect. He was perfect. Love was in the air and her future didn't look so bleak after all.

Ma's eyes crinkled in worry a little bit more when Jess came the next week to take Katy out on another picnic. He didn't come in and visit. He'd catch her out in the field, the barn, or wherever she happened to be and after a hasty goodbye she'd be on the hard wooden seat of the buggy next to him going down the dirt road.

The next couple weeks were much the same. Katy floated around on a cloud and Ma's face became drawn with worry lines. It wasn't that Jess was a bad sort she'd told Katy, but a good man needed to visit with her parents so she could tell if he really was a decent man. Katy laughed at Ma and her antiquated way of thinking. Jess was a perfect gentleman. It'd been their third picnic before he'd kissed her, which Katy had bypassed that bit of information from Ma, not to mention he was her ticket out of there. She wasn't about to argue with Ma, she knew it was useless. She just did her work and every week she'd dream about their picnic to come.

The sweat was dripping from her every pore in the heavy heat the day Rex came back home again. As Katy watched the riders approach from the shade of a tree, she studied the man who rode beside Rex. He was an average looking man, but then again after meeting Jess no man could compare in looks, wit, or charm she thought. She studied Rex more. He looked hardened now. Every time he came back he grew more serious and grim. She knew immediately he wouldn't approve of Jess. She decided then that she wouldn't tell him anymore than necessary.

Sunday came and Katy felt better than she had in years. Rex and his friend, Heck, had been doing the majority of the work around the farm. She'd helped Ma some with the house and did a few things outside, but the back breaking work she was used to wasn't her worry. She took special pains to make sure she was extra pretty today. Jess had started coming to church with Sally Mae's family and he was sure to be there again today. She frowned slightly. Rex was being pushed into going by Ma and the two men were sure to meet. She wasn't sure what to think about that.

As their small white washed wooden church came into view, Katy saw Sally Mae and Jess riding with her parents. Her heart surged with joy. She glanced at Rex as they approached and stopped just out of earshot of her friend. He was watching Jess help Sally Mae down from their wagon with a strange look on his face.

"Don't worry big brother, that's her cousin Jess. He's up from Texas visitin' this week." She couldn't resist goading him a little. In a way she still wanted him and Sally Mae to end up together, but other hand she didn't really care. She had Jess.

"I'm not interested in her. I was jus' wonderin' who the new feller was, in case I'd seen his face on any wanted posters lately." She restrained the urge to stick her tongue out at him like a child. Brothers were so infuriating. She'd all but forgotten his friend who stood near the wagon. She glanced at him for a second, but his face was a mask.

"Jess is not a wanted man. He's very sophisticated and quite a gentleman." Katy watched Jess smile at her as he walked into the church with Sally Mae on his arm. Yes, he was a true gentleman.

"How would you know that?" Rex asked bringing her back to their disagreement.

"Don't sound so overbearin'. I was at her house the day he came to town. You could even take some lessons on bein' a gentleman from him." Heck gave Katy his hand to help her off the wagon.

"See even yer friend has better manners than you." Katy taunted.

"You two sound like a couple of kids. You both need some manners." Ma put in as she yled the way into the church. Katy matched strides with her and the men followed. She was glad Jess had already gone inside and didn't hear Ma's last remark. She might've died of embarrassment.

Katy sat in their usual bench, which was directly behind Sally Mae and Jess. Somehow Rex's friend, Heck, had landed a place next to her. At first she was miffed at his brazen act, but then she caught Jess glancing back often, with a look that surprisingly seemed to register jealously. As soon as service was over she'd have to catch him to explain and warn him about Rex.

After a hearty amen, the congregation began to disperse. Neighbors visited and caught up from the week before. They discussed crops, politics, or whatever struck their fancy. Katy made a bee line for Jess.

"Jess wait up." Katy called to him just as he exited the door. He saw her and stopped as she caught up to him.

"Good morning Katy." He acted cordially. She could only imagine what he was thinking. He smiled his same charming smile, but this time it didn't seem to reach his eyes.

"Jess, I wanted to tell you my brother's back in town. He brought one of his friends back with him."

"So I see."

She narrowed her eyes at him. "I don't think you do. They both have this idea that they're my protectors. I don't know what Rex will say to you, but don't let it bother you whatever it might be. He has no control over me or what I do."

Jess stood there facing her, looking somewhat skeptic. "Are we still goin' for our picnic this week then?"

"Of course. Nothin's changed." He eyed her another minute. "Alright, maybe I should meet him here so he'll be more inclined to be on good behavior." He winked at her. She smiled up at him and took his arm he offered her. It would be alright now she thought.

A small group was gathering around Rex and the Fort Smith Marshal.

"I'm waitin' on one more piece of information, then I have an assignment for you Rattlesnake. I think it'll be best handled without a posse for now. Less men makes you less noticeable." Katy and Jess joined the group just as the marshal was telling Rex about some assignment he was bound to leave out on.

"Somethin' tells me that nothin' would make my brother less noticeable Marshal Fagan." Katy threw in. Rex scowled at her.

"You know Miss Katy, I'm half inclined to think you're right, especially with that rattlesnake danglin' around his head." Fagan grinned up at Rex's hat. "But before he gets too well known out in the territory I need to use him on a special assignment."

"It's not too dangerous I hope." Ma had walked up to the growing group outside of the church.

"Not any more dangerous than any of the others Mrs. Redfern. There's always chances, but nothin' on this one has shown itself to be out of the ordinary." Fagan tipped his hat to her.

"That's somewhat reassurin' Marshal thank you. My boy is very dear to me." Katy couldn't help but smile as Rex squirmed uncomfortably. For once it wasn't her under scrutiny and she enjoyed it.

"Are you ready to go home now Ma?" Rex almost sounded desperate, Katy thought. She couldn't help it. She wanted to laugh at him, her big strong, unshakable brother was somewhat embarrassed.

"I am if the marshal is done with you." Ma told him.

"Go ahead. I'll send one of the boys from town out to get you when I get that final piece in. Good day Mrs. Redfern, it was good to see you again." Rex, Heck, and Ma turned to go to the wagon.

"He doesn't seem so bad." Katy and Jess walked at a slower pace behind the rest.

"He means well, but sometimes he comes off a little too cross."

"It's ok. I can handle him." They'd reached the wagon and he helped her up. Rex gave her a scorching look, but she ignored him and sat down.

The Arkansas River flowed gently under the shimmering scorching sun. The reflection was almost blinding. The trees along the river bank were providing shade for those who sought reprieve from the melting heat of the day. Katy and Jess sat under one such tree enjoying the afternoon.

"I have a question I'd like to ask you Katy." Jess's dark brown eyes looked serious as he sat and faced her squarely.

Sucking in her breath, thinking that the next question was the proposal she'd been waiting on during her short lonely nights, she agreed.

"How badly do you want to leave here?" Well it wasn't what she wanted yet, but they were warming up to it, she thought.

"I can think of barely anythin' but leavin'."

"Would you like to wear the latest style dresses and ride horses?" She was liking the sound of everything coming from his handsome mouth. "Of course I would."

"I have a secret I want to tell you. Can I trust you?"

She nodded emphatically and placed her hand over her heart. "Anything you say I will take to my grave with my lips sealed."

He cocked a crooked grin at her. "Then I have a confession to make." This time it was Katy's turn to get serious. "I don't really have a ranch in Denton." Katy's frown deepened.

"Then how..?" She was momentarily lost for words.

Jess's grinned reached from ear to ear. "I'm an outlaw. A wanted man. But, I have money and if you'll come with me you won't have to work another day in your life. You can wear fancy clothes and not want for anything."

She felt her jaw dropping open in complete shock. She couldn't speak as the impact of his words hit.

"Where are you goin'?" She asked when she finally found her voice. It'd taken her a minute to evaluate how serious he really was. He didn't look like he was joking.

"Indian Territory. I've got some friends there that help me. Best thing about it is I have almost complete immunity to the law as long as we leave the Indians alone."

A thousands things flashed through Katy's mind at once.

"We'll get married on our way there. I'll buy you the prettiest dress you've ever seen. Together we can be rich and in a year or two we can move anywhere you want and live an easy life."

In a way it was her dream come true, but an outlaw? It was risky. Her pulse had shot up and she felt a surge of excitement as she looked down at her dress that was barely more than rags.

"I'll come with you." He pulled her into his arms and kissed her with a passion she reciprocated, fueled by danger and the prospect of adventure.

"I need to make some arrangements for us so give me a lil time and we'll leave soon. Don't let your ma know, she'll try to stop us for sure." He didn't have to say don't tell Rex, that was a given, but it helped he was also out of town. His friend Heck had left a few days before so she didn't have any prying eyes looking over her back. She felt as if she had wings and was finally getting to spread them out and fly.

The more she let the idea grow, the more she embraced it and readied herself to change her way of life.

Over the next few days, Ma must've sensed a change in her. Katy would catch her giving her strange looks that she couldn't decipher. Maybe it was her unusually carefree mood or her skipping steps, but whatever it was she needed to act more normal or Ma would stop her before they could leave.

"Please Sally Mae, you've got to help us." Katy pleaded with her friend. Jess stood next to her silent and strong like her knight.

"I don't know Katy. I think you should at least tell your ma where you're going." Sally Mae said unconsciously toying with the front ruffle of her dress.

"C'mon Sally Mae you know as soon as I do she'll find Rex and he'll stop us before we even have a chance to get married!" Katy was begging her best friend to take her and Jess to the ferry so they could elope.

"We'll be back a couple of weeks and life will be back to normal again. It's jus' a short time." Jess spoke for the first time in their little meeting. Sally Mae still didn't look totally convinced. The three of them stood in the shade a large Mimosa tree out of ear shot of Sally Mae's house.

A midmorning breeze drifted through, cooling the trio to just below the melting point. Jess had picked up Katy a little earlier than their usual time for their picnic that day. She hadn't packed much, mostly because she didn't own much and Jess had promised her new clothes on the trip. Her heart was still beating wildly, hoping Ma didn't become too suspicious before they had a chance to catch the ferry.

"All we want is a chance at happiness. Please Sally Mae you've jus' got to do this for us. You know I'd do it for you." Katy took her friends hands in her own and pleaded with her whole heart.

"Oh ok. I can't stand that pitiful look on your face anymore." Katy nearly squealed with delight and forced herself not to jump up and down like a child. Sally Mae still looked unconvinced.

The horse and buggy were already hitched and ready. Jess helped both women into the seats before he climbed up next to Katy.

Jess flicked the reigns over her horse. The buggy jolted and bounced down the road on carrying them to freedom, to wealth, and to a total new beginning. Katy took in a deep breath of the familiar smells, inhaling them in a whole new way.

"Sally Mae, do you think you could help Katy pick out a couple of dresses? She needs somethin' more suitable that what she's wearin' now." Jess asked as they came to the edges of town.

"Of course. I'd love too!" Sally Mae exclaimed smiling broadly and casting a happy look at Katy who was momentarily speechless.

"I want you to help her pick out something stylish so she'll look sophisticated." Katy thought for a second she should take offense, but she knew all too well she wasn't in the least bit sophisticated in any manner.

"Do you really mean it Jess? I can pick out any dress?" Katy asked him not believing her ears.

"Of course. I want my bride to look her best." He smiled at her. She reached her arms around him the best she could on the bumpy seat and hugged him.

"I so wish you'd stay here and get married. I'd love to be there for it."

"I know Sally Mae and I wish we could do it a different way, but you know what Rex would do or even Ma if they found out before we were actually married. I'd end a spinster for the rest of my life!"

"You ladies go do your shoppin'. I need to go pick up a few things and I'll meet you back here to pay for what you picked out." Jess helped both women down outside of the dress shop situated in the middle of town, with a view of the river from its windows.

Sally Mae took Katy by the hand and led her into the sunlit shop.

"I don't know where to begin." Katy said in awe of the colors and fancily dressed mannequins.

"Good afternoon ladies. Hello again Sally Mae. What can I do for you today?" A woman greeted from the side of the store. Katy turned to look at the speaker and saw a woman who looked elegant in a dress that the hip portion was pulled back with a bubble on her back end. The top was tailored to fit and show off her thin waist line. Sally Mae had similar ones and soon so would she! The woman had her hair neatly pinned in a style she'd often seen Sally Mae use. The woman looked no more than ten years older than herself.

When Sally Mae realized Katy hadn't answered she spoke. "Gladys, my friend Katy here is getting married soon and she needs a couple of dresses of the finest fashion."

The woman looked at Sally Mae as she spoke, then turned her gaze at Katy. She looked her up and down. Katy wanted to squirm under the critical eye of Gladys, but steeled her nerves against the urge. After careful examination of Katy, Gladys turned to Sally Mae.

"Good heavens she's skinny. She doesn't need a corset, but to be properly dressed we should start there." Gladys led the way to the back of the store.

As they began to fit Katy for a corset Gladys measured and clucked her tongue at her, exclaiming things like "such a boyish figure", "your arms are too muscular for a lady", "what dark skin, like a man", and other things that made Katy feel guilty. She knew it was from working their farm like she had. Next time she went dress shopping she hoped she had a more feminine figure so she wouldn't be so humiliated.

Sally Mae stood back and watched Gladys work. "Don't look so sad Katy." She finally said. "Gladys is the best seamstress in town. She'll make you look stunning and Jess won't know what to do with you." That finally brought a smile and half giggle out of Katy.

"Sally Mae's right. I am the best in town and I'll have you lookin' so good, your fella won't even know who you are." Gladys chimed in and she tied off a corset she'd deemed was necessary for Katy.

Over the next hour Katy was measured, layers of skirts were applied, pinned, tucked and fluffed, shirts were buttoned, arms held out, before she was finally allowed to walk in front of the mirror to see her reflection. Katy gasped as she saw herself, not only had she only seen herself in a mirror the size of her hand, but the scared girl she felt inside was staring back at her in the form of a beautiful woman in dark blue dress. The bodice was fitted to her small chest, the bows carefully concealing the hook and eye closures. The skirt was pulled tight to actuate her hips, or in her case give the impression that she had hips, then bunched up and carefully folded over a bustle. The lower tier of the skirt was more bell shaped and the ruffles and trim on it highlighted the femininity of it all.

"Oh my goodness I forgot something." Gladys exclaimed. Katy couldn't take her eyes off the mirror. What could Gladys possibly have forgotten? While Gladys went to get the missing piece, Katy swished her hips back and forth, watching how the skirt swayed gently in the mirror. She felt like such a fine lady.

A minute later Gladys came back and carefully perched a matching blue hat on her head. She could walk by Rex and he wouldn't even recognize her!

She laughed out loud at the thought. Yes, this was the best decision she'd ever made in her life. As Katy changed back into her travelling clothes, she heard Jess come in to pay for the beginning of her new wardrobe.

The smell of stagnant water, dead fish, and hundreds of sweating bodies hung in the air near the Arkansas River. Oh, but it was a beautiful sight. The gentle rippling of the water, the sunlight's blinding reflection from its depths, the way it sighed like a contented lover. She would miss this river. It was where she'd fallen in love with Jess, where she'd made her decision to change her status forever from a poverty stricken near orphan, and where she'd decided to leave her family and become the wife of Jess Whitley.

Stopping the buggy as close to the ferry as she could, Sally Mae held the reigns of her favorite horse. Jess helped both women down, handing Katy her small bag of things she'd managed to sneak out, and her large package containing her new clothing. He lifted a similar smaller package that wasn't as neatly wrapped that he'd bought at the general store.

"Thank you so much Sally Mae. I'll see you after some time." Sally Mae gave her a quick hug and Katy could've sworn she saw the glint of a tear in her eye. She hesitated only briefly before they turned and left.

The gently floating ferry carried the two lovers across the expanse of river. Katy willed herself not to look back, not to second guess her decision as the reality of it briefly hit her. She kept her blue eyes trained on the far shore that grew near. By the time they exited off the ferry into Indian Territory, Katy thought she would faint from excitement. Ma hadn't stopped her. Rex hadn't stopped her. Here she was, standing on the threshold of her new life, she thought as she stepped off the ferry. She looked up into Jess's dark, handsome face. Yes, she was where she should be.

A middle aged man held the reigns of six strong looking horses as he sat atop the driver's seat. He looked rugged thought Katy. He fit the part of a stage driver. Jess helped her into the stage, then before he climbed in behind her he turned to the driver. Not understanding why he wasn't at her heels she paused and looked out the window. Jess slipped the driver what looked like money. Puzzled by this, she momentarily lost her enthusiasm. She wondered if she should ask or just let it go.

"You didn't see us on here." Jess said in a low voice to the driver. The driver took the proffered bill and tucked it away in his pocket. Katy was only beginning to understand the full implications of what kind of journey they were embarking on.

A few short minutes later, with three other travelling companions, the stage lurched onto the dusty, bumpy road bound for... well Katy wasn't sure where they were bound for other than a new life and marriage.

The other passengers were all men, rugged, rough looking men. Katy held back a grimace as she glanced at her travelling companions. They were mostly unshaved and shaggy in varying degrees. Rex looked like that sometimes when he came in

the first day after a trip, but he didn't stay that way
long. These men didn't look like they cared. She
wondered if Jess would look like that soon out here
in the uncivilized land of the Indians. She stopped a
chill before it ran through her body as she thought
about the Indians. Some occasionally drifted into
Fort Smith, but she didn't have personal experience
with them. They mostly kept to themselves. Now it
was different. It appeared she'd be living amongst
them.

CHAPTER 7

"It was excitin' and scary. You know I've never been far from home and here I was with my big dreams headed to the most lawless place in the country. What a fool I was. Rick knew I didn't belong from the moment he laid eyes on me. I wish now he'd have had enough sense to haul me back home instead of trying to argue with Jess." Looking upward, Katy seemed to me searching for answers or maybe she was asking God why He'd let her get into the trouble she had.

Rex opened his mouth to ask who Rick was, but abruptly shut it so she could tell her story her way.

The first stage stop felt like it came quickly, even though it'd only been a couple of hours. They got out and walked around. Jess, the ever present gentleman, took her arm and attempted to shield her from the appreciative eyes of the other passengers.

"Don't worry my dear, we'll be off this stage soon and on our way to your new life." Jess patted her hand that was gently resting on his arm.

"I'm not worried. I'm excited and can't wait." He smiled at her indulgently.

Within half an hour they were back on the stage and bumping along again. The youngest of the three men couldn't seem to keep his eyes off of Katy. She kept hoping Jess would say something to the man, but he didn't. He seemed not to notice her uncomfortable squirm against his arm. Just when she thought she would burst out and scream at the man for staring at her so, she started to talk herself down. Alright Katy, what are you going to do when you get out to this unknown land and men stare at you all the time because you're a white woman? Are you chicken and a coward? I thought you wanted adventure and daring and you can't even handle the stares of one man with Jess seated next to you? What can he do to you now?

Stiffening her spine, she tried her best to ignore the man. He wasn't a bad looking man if she was perfectly honest with herself, but the open examination on his face of her was unsettling.

"Driver. Driver. Stop here." Katy looked at Jess curiously. They were between stage stops and practically in the middle of nowhere. What on earth was he doing telling the driver to stop? She felt the stage slow to a stop. Jess was grinning at her puzzled expression.

"Here's where we get off my dear."

"Here?" Katy risked a quick glance at their travelling companions. They looked as confused as she felt. The oldest looking one looked like he was about to say something to them, but just as quickly clamped his mouth shut.

"Yep. Let's go." He helped her out of the coach and handed her the small bag that her belongings were contained in and her bundle of new clothes. She couldn't wait for the opportunity to wear them. "Alright driver. Go ahead."

Katy watched as a swirl of dust picked up and the stagecoach disappeared from view. She looked around at the gently rolling hills and the stubby brush. This definitely wasn't Arkansas anymore. Sure there were familiar trees and plants, but the whole landscape was different, even the air was different. She felt so alive, maybe even a little skittish, but her rock of strength was with her.

"You gonna stand there and wait for the next stage or you comin' with me?" Jess asked as he walked around the sparse brush.

"I'm comin'." Katy picked up her belongings and followed behind Jess. "Where are we goin' now?"

"Not far from here one of my assistants is supposed to be waiting for us with a couple of horses. After we meet him, we head for home."

"How long will it take us to get there?" Katy had a hundred questions now that they were off the stage. Some of her questions she'd wanted to ask while on the stage, but thought better of it in front of the other passengers, such as when were they to be married? Would they live alone,? She knew he had business partners.

"It's a few days ride. We'll have to camp out a couple of nights."

"Are we goin' to get married on the way or after we get there? Ouch!" In her curiosity she'd neglected to turn her full attention to where she was walking and a thick thorn bush caught her legs and arm.

Jess turned back and gave her a look she couldn't quite read and continued on. She untangled herself from the thorns and scampered to catch up to him. He'd probably not realized he hadn't answered her question so she tried again. "When are we gettin' married?"

"In due time my dear. There're things we must do first." He didn't even look back at her when he answered. He seemed more concerned with the scenery. She accepted his answer at face value before her thoughts turned to what had him so preoccupied. He veered to the right and kept walking.

Katy soon gave up trying to talk to him. He was clearly too preoccupied and she was beginning to wonder if she'd spend the next several days hiking through the woods when the brush opened up to a small clearing.

An old barn stood leaning haphazardly to one side. The charred remnants of what looked like the house were heaped in a pile half way across the clearing from the barn. Poor people, Katy thought, they'd lost their homes, maybe even their lives. She was almost curious enough to go explore the ruins to see if any bodies remained, but just as quickly dismissed the gruesome thought. A blurry memory of herself being carried away from a fire flitted through her mind from her childhood. Fires weren't a thing to be fascinated with, they destroyed people's lives. Look what it had done to her family. It'd sent them to Fort Smith where they had done nothing but work themselves to death.

A strange whistle brought Katy from her reverie. She looked around wondering where it'd come from when she saw Jess making strange faces and the same whistle came out.

"What're you doin'?"

"Callin' Rick."

"What?" Katy was thoroughly confused. Just then a man leading two saddled horses came out of the leaning barn. He was dark, almost clean shaven, sporting a mustache and close cropped dark hair. His features weren't as handsome as Jess and he looked to be shorter.

"I was callin' Rick. He's my right hand. He brought us some horses to ride back so we don't have to walk the whole way."

Rick approached the two on foot. He eyed Katy with a mixture of appreciativeness and skepticism. Katy only squirmed for a second before she remembered her resolve she'd made in the stage coach. If she was going to be the wife of an outlaw, she was going to have to be tough and not easily intimidated. She straightened to her full height as Rick stopped and dismounted.

"Hello Rick. I'm Katy." He managed half a smile with more sneer than good will in it before he turned to face Jess.

"What'd you bring her along for?"

"A man needs a good woman around. Don't look so skeptical. C'mon I'll tell you about it on our way." Jess clapped Rick on the back good naturedly. Rick's eyes glanced around as if making sure they were alone.

"Here, go change into these." Jess turned to Katy and handed her the small bundle that he'd brought from the general store. Thinking it was more pretty clothes that he'd picked out for her, she took the small bundle and scurried off to the barn. When she reached the door she looked back.

"Is it safe to go inside?" She didn't really care who answered. She just needed reassurance that the barn wasn't going to cave in on her when she went in.

"Yes, now hurry." It was Jess who answered and he was acting impatient. He would know. She slipped inside the dimly lit barn. It was devoid of any stalls, boxes, or polls. It was only a shell. She laid the bundle from Jess on the ground and untied it. It looked like men's clothes. Had he given her the wrong bundle? She picked up the pieces of clothing one by one. No, they didn't look like they'd fit anyone but her. She frowned. Why did he want her to wear men's clothes when he'd just bought her two of the most beautiful dresses she'd ever seen? She shrugged and put them on.

Feeling more self conscious than she had at the dress shop, Katy stepped out of the barn. The two men had been sitting astride their horses waiting on her and talking, but when they saw her they stopped. Jess eyed her critically, which was something he'd never done before. Katy's hand toyed with her collar nervously. Finally, he nodded in approval.

"Here put your hair up under this." Jess produced a man's hat and handed to her. She eyed it somewhat skeptically, but took it from him. "C'mon we don't have all day for you to stand there." His tone had become increasing gruff since they'd left Fort Smith. Katy began to wonder if this is how he'd be all the time now. She wasn't sure she liked this side of him.

"Why do you want me to look like a boy?" Katy finally asked as she quickly stuffed her hair under the slightly smelly hat.

"In this territory you don't want to be known as a woman. Sometimes bad things happen to women out here. It's best you don't attract attention to yourself." It sounded reasonable enough.

Mounting the long legged brown horse, she was amazed at how much easier it was in men's pants. She examined her horse from the saddle as they started into the woods. She didn't know much about horses, but she figured if these men really were outlaws that their horses would be fast.

As the horses trotted through the woods, Katy briefly wondered what Ma would say if she saw her now sitting astride a horse and riding like a man. Maybe if she was going to ride a lot like this she should ask Jess to buy her some men's pants. She smiled at the thought. How ridiculous she looked wearing men's pants and looking like a boy! She stopped herself from laughing out loud.

The next few hours were passed in relative quiet. They stopped as little as possible to take a break and water the horses. Katy had a hundred questions she wanted to ask, but something in the men's mannerisms held her back.

As the sun began to dip low in the west and the shadows started to meld into one, the trio stopped in a small clearing to make camp. Katy almost fell into Jess's arms when she dismounted her horse.

"Whoa there, Katy." Jess caught her from falling to the ground. "I thought you were tougher than that."

"Sorry, Jess. I haven't been on a horse for that long in a long time." She looked into his face in the fading light for a sign of tenderness or sympathy. What she saw was a luke warm expression that she couldn't quite read. She'd expected more warmth and tenderness, for a second she was afraid. As she rubbed her aching muscles, Jess walked away to start on camp. She decided he was putting on a front for Rick since he hadn't seemed too happy she was along. Just then she caught Rick giving her a contemptuous look. She dropped her hands and knew she couldn't show any signs of weakness.

At first Katy was at a loss as to what she should do. She thought she was doing pretty good just to stand up. Jess and Rick had set about making camp like they did it all the time together. She caught herself before she frowned at the thought. What was she getting herself into again? If Ma ever found out, it would be a humiliation Ma couldn't bear. Katy straightened her stiff shoulders the best she could. Ma could live with barely nothing, she, however, could not.

Holding the reigns of her mount, still at a loss as to what she should be doing at that moment, Jess came back to her. He put his arms around her and kissed her forehead. She leaned into his warmth and strength.

"You've had a rough day out, my bride. Relax tonight while we set up camp. Tomorrow night you can help." As Jess stepped back from her, she thought she might collapse. She was used to farm work, but the excitement and travel had her exhausted. She started to look around for a place to make herself comfortable when she caught Rick glaring at her again from the shadows at the edge of camp. She didn't have the energy to analyze Rick's cynicism tonight, nor did she care too much just now. Jess's attitude toward her had softened since they'd stopped. Maybe he'd been nervous earlier. She wasn't sure, but the fears that she'd built up were dissipating again.

Katy unsaddled the horse she'd rode that day and after tying it out to graze, she sat on a soft pile of leaves and leaned against the saddle. She hadn't realized she nodded off until Jess nudged her as he sat down beside her. He offered her a plate of food.

"It might not be fine dining, but it's grub anyway." She smiled at his shadowed face. The light from the fire being the only visible light in the darkness that had descended while she'd slept. She took the plate and ate hungrily. Jess sat quietly next to her eating his own meal. Rick sat on a rock on the opposite side of camp from them. He still didn't look too friendly

After they ate, Jess produced a bedroll for each of them. He laid them out with only a short distance between them. As Katy lay down, she felt a nervous excitement being in this close of sleeping quarters to the love of her life. For a fleeting moment she wondered what it would be like once they were finally married and sharing a bed. Then as the quiet descended on the camp, she laid there staring up at the stars and wondered if the Indians would kill them in their sleep. Surely they wouldn't be hurt, after all Jess had lived out there before. But what if wolves came? She shivered at the thought. What if a rattlesnake came to share her bed? She gripped her arms with her hands crossed over her body trying to stop the shaking that had started with her compounded fears.

She glanced over at Jess to see if he saw her fears, but he appeared to be sleeping peacefully. She couldn't see Rick from her position, not that it mattered, but she really didn't want him to see how scared she felt. She could tell he resented her presence there. Turning her eyes back to the heavens, Katy wondered if she'd be able to sleep at all.

The next morning Katy jerked awake as birds' chatter filled the air. It was already morning. She needed to get started on her chores. She started to sit up. No, she didn't have chores any more. Her life had changed as of yesterday. She looked around camp, surprised she'd fallen asleep so quickly last night despite her fears, but saw no one. The fire was smoking, but there was no sign of the men. For a panicked second she considered the thought that Jess had left her alone in Indian Territory. She thought to call out for him, but thought better of it. He wouldn't just leave her. They were to be married soon. With renewed strength, she rolled up her bedroll and tied it to her horse. She walked over to investigate the fire. A pot of coffee was waiting for her.

Katy was sitting on a rock, enjoying the coffee, when Jess rode in. "I see yer finally up sleepyhead." He smiled at her as he stopped a few feet away.

"If ya didn't want me sleepin' so long, ya shoulda woke me up."

"It's alright. We've got another long day ahead of us. All I did was bring back a squirrel for us to eat on today." He said, as he held up a fat, dead squirrel by the tail.

"Oh good. Should I cook it before we leave?"

"Might as well, otherwise it'll spoil." Jess left the squirrel with her and turned back to his horse.

After two more days of rugged travel, they came upon a small rough hewn log house that was tucked away into the landscape, unnoticeable to an untrained eye. The way the men approached it was more like they were walking up to a rattlesnake than a house. Jess and Rick left her out of sight while they went to check out the house. She didn't mind too much. She was tired of travelling and was glad for a chance to stop. Her muscles were just barely getting used to the long hours on a horse, but she was still painfully sore.

She had tried to do her part on the trail helping with camp. Jess had almost imperceptively alternated between being his usual charming self with her and holding her slightly aloof. She wondered if he still wasn't sure how to act around her with Rick still glaring at her from the shadows. She had tried to ignore him, she had tried to be nice to him, but he remained impassive.

"C'mon Katy. Come see your new home." Jess motioned for her to follow him a few minutes later when he returned with a grin on his face. Katy smiled back. Her new home, those words had such a welcome ring to her ears.

They stopped their horses at the hitching post and tied them up, which Katy wondered if it was necessary since their horses seemed to be well trained. She looked at the small little cabin and wondered if she would faint. It didn't seem possible. Was she still dreaming? She had her own house with the handsomest man she knew. She wouldn't be hearing any disapproval from her brother or Ma. She could do as she pleased and Jess had told her she wouldn't have to work from dawn till dusk like she had been doing for so long.

"You must be happy the way you're smilin'." Jess walked up to her as she stood just outside the door and gathered her into his arms. Katy sensed an underlying hunger in his kiss that she hadn't felt before, or maybe it was the setting, she wasn't sure, but it made her nerves tingle more.

As Jess's kiss became more demanding, Katy pulled back. "What 'bout Rick? What will he say?"

She would be so embarrassed if he came up on them.

"Don't worry 'bout him. He's gone on." That's when she realized she hadn't seen him after he and Jess had gone ahead to check out the house. Jess took her hand and led her into the small house. She barely had a chance to look around at her new living quarters when Jess resumed him earnest kissing.

Her head reeled with the excitement and sensations that were so new to her. Before she knew what was happening Jess had half her shirt unbuttoned, as she was still wearing the boy's clothes. When she realized what he'd done, she pushed him back again, only to have him grab her back.

"Wait Jess, we're not even properly married yet." She said breathlessly.

"Don't worry we will be." He pressed his lips against hers again and started to make his way down her neck.

"It's not proper for us to be doin' this yet." Katy pleaded breathlessly again, more feebly this time as she again tried to step back from him.

He stopped and held her shoulders as he looked into her eyes in the fading light. "Look Katy, out here, things aren't always *proper* like you think of them as being. Civilized people are far and few between and the ones that are around ain't exactly concerned with propriety. We'll get married some time, but right now I'm not sure when that'll be. But that doesn't have to stop us from livin' as a man and wife now."

Katy wasn't sure she really understood, but who would know? Who would stop them? Nobody. Jess didn't give her a chance to think about consequences or propriety. He took her as his unwed wife. She didn't resist.

CHAPTER 8

"I should've known then things weren't as they seemed, but I was still blind. I believed the lies. I didn't want to not believe them, because I knew if I were honest with myself I couldn't stay." She was retreating inside herself, the strength she'd shown when she'd began her story was waning.

Rex scooted closer and put a hand on her shoulder encouraging her on. Her shoulders sagged under the weight of his hand as if a small weight had been placed there.

A grey light filled the eastern horizon. It was the first day of her new life and she wasn't sure where to start. She was so used to her routine at home that she was unsure of what her duties were now. Her body felt sore. She went to sit up and get out of bed. Maybe she shouldn't get out of bed just yet. No, she reasoned with herself, she needed to get up and get Jess his breakfast started. He would expect that of his wife. Soundlessly she got out of bed.

Smiling to herself, she went into the kitchen to see what she could cook. This would be a nice change from her life before. No back breaking work outside. Just keep the house up and keep him happy. It sounded so simple. No standing over a hoe all day. No splitting fire wood to keep the house warm. No ragged dresses. Yes, she could get used to this kind of life.

Finding a candle that was nearly completely used, she managed to light it as she fumbled around the kitchen trying to learn her way around in the dim light.

"Good morning." Katy almost squealed at Jess's voice behind her. She spun to face him, ready to scold him for sneaking up on her, but one look at him with his hair all tousled, and his sleepy smile, kept the words from coming out of her mouth.

"Did you sleep good?" She asked, not sure how a woman should approach a man after they had been so intimate.

"Very well actually. How 'bout you?" He asked as he closed the distance between them and swept her into his arms, kissing her soundly on the lips. After returning his kiss, she pulled back enough to look up at him.

"So did I. What should I make for your breakfast?" She was lost in this new place. There was little food to be found.

"A cup of coffee and you." Jess answered giving her a seductive smile. It was like a dream come true. She couldn't help but smile back.

"Surely you need some nourishment?"

"Not this early." His expression became more serious. "I have to ride out soon. I'll give you three days to make this house how you like it, then we'll start your schoolin',"

"My schoolin'?" She asked as he released her and reached for the jar of coffee beans.

"Yes. If you're goin' to become of any use you need to know certain things." Katy was puzzled. Would he school her in things a wife should know to be a good wife for her husband?

"I'll be back by sundown." He gave her a quick peck then left, a pot of coffee boiled on the stove. She watched his retreating figure before she turned back to the kitchen, looking at it in a whole new light. This was her new life. Her house. Her kitchen. Her husband.

Just as she went to take the coffee off the stove, Jess reappeared. He took the proffered cup she offered him and drank it in two scalding gulps.

"I'll make sure milk and eggs are brought to you today." With that he walked back out the door. A minute later she heard hoof beats leaving the house. She was alone. Again.

She surveyed her surroundings. Where did she even begin? She was still sore from the journey out here or was it from becoming a wife? With that thought she realized she felt dirty, a different kind of dirty than she was used to. If Jess was going to be gone all day, maybe she should start with a bath.

Surely there was a well near the house. It might chase away some of the aches and give her time to figure out what to do first.

By late morning Katy had bathed and felt as if she could conquer the world. Realizing she didn't have any rags to clean with, she ripped up her work dress that she'd worn practically every day for.. well she couldn't remember how long. She wore the men's clothes that Jess had her wear on their journey since she couldn't see herself wearing her new fashionable clothes to clean the house. As she ripped up the threadbare dress she wondered why Jess had her buy new clothes, and fancy ones at that, if she was going to live out here in the middle of nowhere.

The next few hours went by in a blur as she dusted and scrubbed the little house, preparing it for her new role as a wife.

"Whitey didn't tell me what a pretty girl you were." Katy whirled around slinging soapy water across the room as she stood facing the sound of the voice near the door of the cabin, suppressing the urge to scream at being taken completely off guard. In the doorway stood a man, or rather a boy considering he looked not much than a day older than she, with shaggy blonde hair and an impish grin.

"Who are you and what do you want?" Katy asked warily realizing she was alone with a strange man in an unfamiliar land.

"I am Clayton Roger Darby, one of Whitey's trusted associates." He explained, doffing his hat almost mockingly. "Most folks call me Clay. Jess came by earlier and asked me to find a milk cow for ya and bring it over. So here I am and there's yer cow." He pointed across the yard to a brown dairy cow munching grass like it belonged there.

"Oh, thank you." Katy smiled to herself. It was nice having someone look out for her. Too late she realized she was smiling at Clay. The way he smiled back he must've taken her gratitude the wrong way.

"Anythin' you need, you jus' ask me and I'll see that you get it." The smile he gave her said that his offer extended beyond bringing her cows.

"Thank you, but I have Jess for that." Her curt reply didn't do much to take the leer off his face as a flicker of amusement crossed his face, but he backed down all the same. She'd have to get used to him being called Whitey by his friends, but it still sounded so strange to her.

"So you do, so you do. Well miss, I'm sure I'll be seein' you soon." With that he tipped his shabby hat and disappeared into the woods.

Only after she was able to convince herself that she was alone once again did Katy move from the spot her feet felt frozen too and exhaled a sigh of relief she didn't realize she'd held. She walked out and took care of the cow wondering if this was what she'd have to face on a regular basis and fervently hoped Jess would be around more.

As hoof beats sounded near the little cabin just before sundown, a jolt of fear jumped into her throat. Was Clay returning? Was it some other unknown *associate* of Jess's that approached? Maybe it was Jess himself? Better to know what was coming at her before it got there. She peered out the window from the side of the house the hoof beats came.

It was Jess. Dropping her dirty rag where she stood, Katy ran out of the house to greet him. He saw her running toward him and dismounted his horse.

"I'm so glad you're home." She all, but collapsed into his arms with relief.

"Has you're day been that tryin' or you jus' miss me that much?" He teased before kissing her soundly on the lips.

She wasn't sure if she should admit how scared she'd been the whole day alone in an unknown area, especially after Clay's visit, or not. She didn't want him to think she was too weak to be his wife.

"I jus' missed you that much," she said opting for flattery and burying her own fears.

"Go get dinner started while I put Jack out to graze. We've had a long ride." Jess turned to walk away then paused and turned back. "By the way did Clay come over with a cow today?"

"Yes he did." Katy wondered if she should bring up the way Clay gave her the creeps, but then the moment was gone.

"Good." And that was all that was said of the matter.

Long before the third day arrived, Katy had everything arranged, cleaned, and ready for their adventure together. She thought.

As the grey light of dawn seeped in the windows of the third day, Katy resisted the urge to jump out of bed and start working. She didn't have to. There was nothing for her to do today. She'd finished it all before lunch the day before. She rolled over and wrapped her arms around Jess.

"Good mornin'. What will you do today?" Jess's rough morning voice greeted her. He rolled over to face her, kissing her nose, the beginnings of his unshaved face prickled her skin.

"I'm not sure."

"Would you like to ride with me today?"

Katy smiled brightly. "Sure."

"It wouldn't hurt for you to get used to the saddle. We'll have a lot of days we'll live in the saddle. Tomorrow we begin your trainin'." Katy cocked her eye brow at him.

It sounded exciting. She was ready. This place was just as quiet at the farm back home, maybe even more so. There was nobody around. The only other person she'd seen since she'd arrived was Clay.

Once again, she dressed in her boy clothes as she had everyday this far. Her old work dress had seen its last day as she'd cleaned the house. Her finer dresses Jess had bought before coming hung in their room, waiting for something, she just wasn't sure what.

They rode out at a leisurely pace side by side. The silence that enveloped them was comfortable enough. Katy was happy just being out. She wasn't plowing fields, harvesting, raking hay, or any of the farm work. She was taking a leisurely ride with her husband, well almost husband. This was the type of life she'd dreamed about.

Before half the morning had passed, they were riding up to an average looking cabin. A few stray livestock wondered the yard. A child, that Katy guessed to be near ten, stared at them holding a chicken she'd caught. She was barefoot and only a small wisp of a thing. Katy thought she must've looked like that at her age. She was about to turn to Jess and ask him who lived there when a man of similar wiry stature to the child walked out. He had a touch of grey in his dark hair and beard.

"Whitey you ol' devil. You come up here to put me back in business?" The man grinned and held out his hand to Jess, only then did he seem to realize that a woman rode beside him. "Who's this?"

Turning her attention to Jess she watched his reaction. He was smiling at the man congenially. "Morgan, meet my wife Katy. She's new to the area and is goin' to help me in our *business.*"

Morgan's green eyes crinkled at the edges as he grinned at Katy. "Nice to meet you Katy." His rough hand encompassed hers as he shook her hand also. "I just started some coffee inside. Wanna cup?"

Jess took the offer and they dismounted. The young girl had disappeared with the chicken.

Walking into the small cabin was much like walking into her own new cabin. Sparse. It definitely lacked a woman's touch. Was there a woman to tend to the girl? She wanted to ask but was unsure if she should interrupt the men's conversation, which she hadn't been listening to at all. As that realization dawned on her, she turned her focus to them.

"Are you sure she can do it Whitey? I mean that's quite a deal for someone so inexperienced." Morgan said shooting a quick look at Katy, though he tried to mask it. Were they talking about her? Doing what?

"I think in a week or two I can teach her 'bout anything. She's got a strong back and a quick mind." Jess told him reassuringly. What on earth were they discussing? Something she was going to do? Suddenly she felt remote, like an outsider looking in. What did Jess have in mind for her? "Speaking of which, what you gonna do with the girl?"

"Ginny? I'm not sure jus' yet. I'm the only family she's got left after the uprisin' and all. She's too young to take on our business trips." Morgan's concern for the young girl's wellbeing touched Katy. She wished she'd had a caring uncle to step in and fill her own pa's shoes but that wasn't possible, her only know uncle died before Pa.

"What 'bout lettin' her stay with Pale Moon? She would probably take her in, at least temporarily."

"Even if she's only half injun, she's still injun, and looks it too! I don't think Ginny will do it. She'll be scared half to death jus' lookin' at her after what happened to her folks." Morgan argued. Jess didn't look convinced. What happened to Ginny's family? Had they been taken prisoners? Or worse, killed in an uprising like Morgan first suggested?

"It'd be good for her to see that not all injuns are the same. A few days or couple weeks with Pale Moon and she'd forget she was even in an injuns presence."

"I'll think on it. If'n she agrees I'll let you know at the meetin' next week." Morgan's scruffy countenance was twisted in deep concentration.

The conversation drifted to less obscure subjects and within the hour they were headed back toward home. The little girl, Ginny, never reappeared leaving Katy pondering her fate. Only later that day did she realize it was her own fate she should have been questioning.

CHAPTER 9

"Rex?" Katy's sad eyes found his.

"Yeah?" His voice came out gruffer than he expected. He felt bad for the kid. She was like one of the many he was supposed to be protecting.

"After this is all over, tell me we'll find a way to help Ginny. Morgan's not so bad, but that poor girl can't keep livin' like that. She needs a woman in her life, a woman who really cares for her. She's like the sister or maybe daughter I'll never have. I know I'm not the best example, well not in the last several months, but I know I can do good by her."

"What about Morgan? He's her uncle. Don't you think he'll have somethin' to say about it?" Rex cocked an eyebrow at his sister.

"He knows she needs somethin' better and more stable than he's givin' her. He's a reasonable man. I hope we can work somethin' out that works out best for her."

The sincerity in her voice nearly had him convinced to help her in her endeavor, but her own fate was still to be decided. He wasn't surprised by her plea. Katy had to have the biggest heart he knew, well except for Ma. Katy was a peacemaker and healer by nature. When he and his older brothers would get into a scuffle, Katy would beg and plead with them until they called a truce.

Little streams ran crazily through the yard. Rain had turned the landscape a dull grey, and its ominous voice echoed in Katy's head again, telling her to get out while she still could. She pushed those thoughts aside.

For the first time, in possibly her whole life, she actually felt like a woman, not another man working in the fields. Jess treated her like the woman she longed to be. Over the last few days he'd repeatedly held her and caressed her telling her how beautiful she was and how they were going to ride into a wealthy future together.

Sitting down in a chair near the window, Katy rubbed her sore feet, staring out at the haze that looked much like her own mind. Scenes from the past week played through her mind. Tottering on her beautiful, new fancy shoes in her dresses of the newest fashions she'd felt like a kid dressing in her mother's clothes. It almost felt surreal. She was pretty sure she'd walked a hundred miles in those shoes by the way her feet felt, not to mention her ribs from adjusting to the constriction of the corset that was deemed a necessity by polite society.

An image of Jess sitting in this same chair, elbows on his legs, his face buried in his hands out of frustration because her uneducated speech was like a rock that not even she could move.

Another more frightening image of Jess appeared in her mind. His face was contorted in a menacing, almost wrathful, expression as he had bedded her a few days ago. She'd been trying so hard, but he'd thrown up his hands in exasperation and all but dragged her to bed. She felt as if he'd been taking out his frustrations on her. She'd hid her fear of him then in hopes of preventing a repeat. It seemed the more she acted weak and unwilling the more he acted the brute. There was no place for weakness with him.

Only once this week had she let herself give in to her doubts and fears, after laying awake for hours staring into the darkness after he'd slept. She had cried her eyes out. The next morning he'd looked at her face, without a word he walked out of the house and not come back in until nearly lunch.

The dreariness that hung over the land today seemed to bring out the despair and doubts that'd she'd been hiding most of the week. Inhaling a deep breath, she squared her shoulders and sat up straight. Hopefully after the meeting tomorrow and their *business* venture got underway, he'd soften and she'd be happy again. Were all women treated this way by their men and still managed to act happy? Ma had always adored Pa. She couldn't remember a time when he'd raised his voice or his hand to her. Katy shook her head. It didn't make sense.

Maybe the rain would last a few days, postpone the meeting, and she would have more time to learn her part. Up till now her part had only been acting like a high bred lady. She now had gloves to cover her calloused hands and the day before Jess had produced rice powder for her to lighten her face so she didn't look quite so manly from being out in the sun so much.

Worrying about what was or wasn't to be was not lifting her spirits or getting Jess's coffee ready for him. Forcing herself from the chair and turning her eyes from the window, Katy set off to the kitchen.

A yellowed map lay open on the table that the five men and Katy had gathered around. Jess was pointing and talking with pencil in hand, drawing imaginary lines and discussing possible dangers as Katy just stood there staring, excitement and fear stirred her senses.

Looking around the group she wondered how they all managed to work together. Rick still glared at her with his dark eyes like she was an unwanted guest. Clay shot her, what he probably thought, unnoticed admiring glances from under his shaggy blonde hair. If she hadn't been standing between Jess and Morgan she would've squirmed, but these two made her feel secure. Jess was her protector and Morgan was beginning to seem more like a favorite uncle. Then there was Pete. She knew nothing about him and was completely impartial to him. He'd come in like the others traipsing mud from his boots across the floor. He was every bit as tall as Jess, mostly nondescript wheat colored hair and smoky blue eyes, his face was mostly covered in a growing beard. He couldn't have been much older than Katy or Clay by more than a year or two at that.

"Pete, yer uncle is keepin' mine and Katy's horses for us right?" Pete nodded. Katy's mind flipped back to the conversation at hand. She was about to miss vital information.

"Alright. Make sure nobody knows any of you know each other. If anythin' goes wrong Rick is the only one who is to be contacted until I get there. See ya'll in Dallas in two weeks." Jess looked each man in the eyes one last time before the group dispersed.

Katy stood there silently as she watched the men slowly drift away from the table talking in pairs. Part of her was still frozen in shock at what she'd agreed to become. Part of her argued that this was the only choice she had and she should make the best of it.

"Ginny's gonna stay with Pale Moon." Katy heard Morgan tell Jess. He sounded hesitant and she turned to see the expression on his face. Morgan's face looked strained. Jess put a hand on his shoulder.

"Don't worry about her. She'll be fine." Jess encouraged. Katy didn't see how Jess could say that knowing what Ginny had been through already. She felt sorry for the little girl.

"I'm tryin' not to."

"Don't let it interfere with yer work Morgan. All of our lives are in danger if it does." Jess pinned Morgan with a fierce look. Katy thought her heart would stop when the severity of Jess's words penetrated.

"I won't Jess. I know the consequences."

Jess patted Morgan's shoulder. "I know you won't let us down." Morgan turned to leave. Pete was the last of the men who remained. The others had quietly slipped out the door. Katy stood rooted in place, invisible as Jess and Pete discussed the arrangements with the horses.

Katy turned and walked away. She couldn't take anymore right now or she thought she might completely panic. Never in her life had she done anything near this daring or illegal. She couldn't even go against her own parents let alone the law. What was she doing?

Walking toward the barn, which in reality looked more like a make shift shed to milk the cow, Katy remembered what brought her here to start with. She didn't have to do a man's work any longer and soon she'd have money to buy things she'd never dreamed she'd be able to buy before. Would it be worth the risk? Yes, it would she decided as she pushed the fears out of her mind. She tethered Bessie to the post and began milking her.

"Good girl Bessie." Katy patted the cow's course brown hair soothing her. "I'm so glad I don't have to spend my day out here in the barn, not that I mind you that is, but the work when it's only you to take care of it all is too much." The gentle splashing of the milk collecting in the bucket lent a hand to her melancholy mood. "This whole *business* has got me nervous. I mean Rex is a marshal, what if he finds out what I've been doin'? And even worse catches me? He'll tell Ma for sure after he throws me in that dungeon they call a jail! They might even hang me."

The streaming milk became more intense as Katy's panicked voice rose in pitch. "But if we can pull off a couple of these *business ventures*," she refused to even say the word robbery, feeling like that would immediately curse and doom her, "I'll be able to live like a real lady. I won't have to plow the field or wear men's clothes or break my back everyday like I did at home." Her panic had subsided as she dreamed about fancy clothes and houses where other people did the outside work while she sipped lemonade.

Abruptly her dreams were cut short when she realized that Bessie had given her all she was going to today. With the milk pail half full, Katy started towards the cabin realizing she'd just spent the whole time talking to the cow. She missed having Sally Mae nearby, but she hoped one day they might return to Fort Smith. She sighed wondering how life had become so complicated.

Mixtures of reds and golds colored the gently rolling landscape. It was gentle and inviting. The air was pleasantly warm. The nights had even started cooling. For the first time in years, Katy wasn't dreading autumn. Instead, she sat astride her horse, in a most unladylike pose in her men's clothes, smiling like she owned the world. And she felt like it too.

"You're lookin' very pleased my dear." Jess remarked smiling one of his winsome smiles at her. He held his horse to pace with hers.

"I am. I'm not out in the fields harvestin' or plowin'. I'm here with you and lookin' forward to life for the first time in... well I can't remember when."

His smile deepened. "I don't intend to disappoint you either."

Katy let the whisper of the breeze caress her face and any fear of their journey be carried off by it. Jess was being pleasant again, the brief ruthlessness that had surfaced was gone.

Over the next several days, Katy hid her fears, focusing on the beautiful landscapes and her time with Jess. But each night her dreams were the same. Rex had caught her. Sometimes he was dragging her off to jail in irons, sometimes she was facing the rope with only Ma standing at the foot of the gallows with the same pain on her face as the day Pa died, and sometimes she was sitting in a rat infested cell alone, cold, and in rags. She would wake up sweating in the middle of the night, put an arm across Jess for comfort and try to think of all the leisure's money could buy instead.

By the time they camped outside of Dallas, before her debut, she was jumping at shadows and more skittish than a day old calf.

"Katy, focus on what I'm sayin'." Jess commanded firmly. He sat on a rock directly in front of her. She had just jumped at a shadow for the fourth time in almost as many minutes. With great effort she turned her face to Jess. His calculating brown eyes helped still her fears, for a moment.

"I'm listenin' Jess."

"No, I don't think you are. If you blow this job I'll put you on a train and send you back to Arkansas." His eyes had narrowed as they studied her. "What's wrong with you anyway? You've barely been yourself this whole trip."

Straightening her back, Katy stared back at him. His threat hanging in the air sounded more like something a naughty child would be told, not a wife. She doubted he would do it, but just the same she didn't want to blow her chances for a better life.

CHAPTER 10

"I never realized how much our poverty had affected me. I became greedy. I can't remember a time that I ever let greed guide my life until I met Jess. He convinced me there was nothin' better in life than fancy clothes and things money could buy. I finally felt like somebody. My confidence grew. I learned how to lie and not get caught. I learned that money talks louder than people. It opens doors you never knew existed." Katy's mouth twisted in a grimace.

Silently Rex sat there, his hand still on her shoulder, willing her comfort as he watched the torment play across her face of who she was and who she'd become wrestle with the other.

Clad in her most becoming blue dress with matching hat perched coquettishly atop her head,

Katy strode into the bank like the wealthy lady she dreamed of becoming.

Pausing only for a moment to let her eyes adjust to the inside light, Katy fingered her reticule dangling at the wrist of her gloved hands. For a brief second it seemed every eye in the room found her at once. The men's glances were far more approving than the women's. Gathering her courage around herself like her skirts, Katy walked forward. Only two tellers held the counter, both were occupied. Katy stood in line, doing her best to look aloof when in truth she felt like the walls had eyes and were watching her.

"Can I speak with your superior?" Katy asked in a low tone as if the walls had ears when she stepped up to the teller. His face was a mix of admiration and skepticism. "I have some valuables that I would like to see about depositing in your bank. I'm very cautious about keeping them anywhere but on me, but my dear brother insists I must do so for my own health."

"Give me a moment madam." The teller walked off to a side room where Katy could just make out the corner of a desk, probably where the owner kept his books during the day.

Not a minute after the teller had disappeared into the side room than a man with graying hair and somewhat substantial girth emerged, followed by the teller.

"Good mornin' Miss..." He paused realizing he didn't know her name. He stopped just short of her. He stood well over six inches taller than her. She felt as if his blue eyes could see right through her and covered her fear with a dazzling smile that she had practiced everyday on the long ride there.

"Miss Greene." Katy supplied for him offering her gloved hand.

"I am Thomas Franklin and the owner of this bank. Vince here tells me you have some important business to discuss with me?"

"Good morning Mr. Franklin. It's nice to meet you. Could we speak about my affairs privately?"

"Please, my office is over here." He motioned to the room he'd just exited. She followed him into his office. He held out a chair for her. She sat, arranging her blue skirts around her, keeping her reticule in her lap.

"I have some valuables and some money that I would like to deposit in your bank. I think. I've been skeptical about leaving them with any other person than myself, but my dear brother insists it would be better for my health to have them safely locked away in the bank." She gripped the reticule tighter.

"I see. And you're wondering if my facilities are safe enough from the riff raff to keep them here, is that it?"

"Putting it bluntly, yes."

"Miss Greene, allow me lay your fears to rest." He stood from the wooden, well carved and cushioned chair he'd taken across from her. He walked behind her to what looked to be a closet-like door. On the door was a lock with numbers on a dial holding it tightly shut. It was the first time she'd even seen a combination lock. She stood from her chair and moved closer. The cautious banker turned his back to her, trying to inadvertently shield her from seeing the combination. Standing to the side as if admiring the art on the wall, Katy watched his swift hand turn the dial, pausing for a brief second on each number. Turning her head away as the lock sprang open she focused on memorizing the numbers until he spoke again.

"This is the latest invention to keeping your valuables safe. The lock is a set of numbers that only I know, so any criminal mischief that presents itself can only get in with these numbers. The walls are also of double thickness to prevent any other entry." He said holding the heavy metal lock on his fingers. He opened the small door revealing a shelved interior of neatly stacked bundles of money and boxes with little locks on them.

Removing a small metal box that had a number engraved on the top, he removed a key ring from his pocket full of small keys and opened the box. "You may place your valuables in here and I will give you the key for this box. The only one who can open this box is you, as there is only one key made for this particular box. It will go back into the wall vault and be safe from any unscrupulous characters."

"Mr. Franklin, you are splendid. You've convinced me to bring my valuables here. I will return home at once and tomorrow I will return with them. That lock is a marvelous invention."

"Glad I could be of assistance to you Miss Greene. I look forward to our next meeting."

"Thank you Mr. Franklin. Good day." Without a second glance over her shoulder, Katy left the bank.

Only after she'd turned off the main street and into an alley did she take a deep breath and allow herself to breathe. She almost got lost as she wove between building looking for the livery where Jess was to meet her. Slipping into the side door, Katy would've been glad to collapse into Jess's arms had his face not been so anxious at her arrival.

Glancing around to make sure no passerby had popped in, Jess took hold of her shoulders and looked at her intently. "What'd you find out? Can we do it?"

"We can do it. It's a combination lock in the banker's office. I don't think he lives there. The numbers are twenty one, eleven, twenty eight." She blurted out before she forgot them. "There's other small boxes in the vault that people keep valuables in that only have one key and the banker doesn't have a spare."

"That doesn't matter, we can figure out something. You're terrific, Katy," Jess said as he swooped her up into a fiery kiss fueled by excitement. Katy let herself be swept up into the moment as all her senses seemed to leave her at once.

The streets were filled with raucous laughter and the stench of rot gut whiskey filled the air as the sun dipped deeper into the horizon. A light breeze lifted the wisps of hair that escaped the hat concealing her golden hair and sent a nervous chill down her back. She no longer was dressed in her finery, but had traded it in for her men's garb.

Passing a store window, Katy stopped for a moment to study her reflection. She was startled to realize she looked like a young boy, not a woman, not a man, but a kid. Her small stature with practically no womanly curves and the ill suited clothes lent itself to her masquerade. She wasn't sure if she should be glad she was less likely to be identified as a woman and therefore her true identity unknown, or if it would be more hazardous playing the role of a man in this dangerous business. The gun belt Jess insisted she wear would only invite the trouble she feared, but it was too late to go back now.

Pushing through the double doors into the smoke filled air of the saloon, Katy fought back the urge to cough and gag as the putrid smells of bad alcohol and dirty men filled her senses. Glancing around to see if any of the others had taken their places yet, she found she was the last to join the party. She took up a position at the end of the bar.

"What'll it be?" A burly barkeeper appeared before her. His squinty eyes under bushy brows made her squirm in her chair.

She took a quick nervous glance around. If she didn't take a drink she'd stick out like a preacher in this crowd. She couldn't afford the attention. She was nervous enough as it was. Even Jess wasn't supposed to act like he recognized her.

"Whiskey," she told him in the best man voice that she could muster. The barkeeper only paused a second before turning to get her drink.

Her whiskey appeared before she had time to blink, or so she thought. She glanced around, unsure of what she was supposed to be doing. She'd never stepped foot in a saloon before, let alone dare to peek through the doors. The stale smells of smoke and unwashed bodies mixed with the bawdy music and laughter from the colorfully dressed women of the place made her stomach flop over and her head reel. She realized the barkeeper was still watching her, probably wondering why she hadn't picked up her glass.

It looked as if she'd have to drink the whiskey too.

The smell was almost too much as the glass passed beneath her nose. She closed her eyes and took a sip. The burning ran down her throat and into her butterfly filled stomach. Her eyes flashed opened at the same time her mouth did. She quickly clamped a hand over her mouth to hide her shock. It was the most awful thing she'd ever tasted.

No one else seemed to notice her ignorant display, no one except the barkeeper who'd been carefully watching her from under his bushy brow.

"What're you doin' in a place like this kid? Ain't you got no family?" The barkeep asked her.

"Ain't none of yer business." Katy wasn't trying to be rude, but she was panicking.

"Take my advice kid, go home to where ever it is and stay outta places like this for a few more years. It ain't no place for kids."

Katy was too stunned to say anything. All she could do was glare at him. With determination born out of desperation, she reached for her glass, continuing to keep eye contact with the barkeeper, and downed the rest of her whiskey. It burned like fire, but she'd been prepared for it this time. She barely grimaced. The barkeeper shook his head and walked down the bar to refill the drinks.

Another lurch and a roll later, Katy's stomach started to settle down. The air was getting warm. She tugged at the collar of her shirt. She glanced around again wondering how long it would be until it was time to make their move.

She didn't have long to wait. Pete left his card game after gathering his few remaining chips and soon disappeared out the double doors. Clay must've noticed because he started unwinding the painted woman's arms from around his neck and said his goodbyes to her. Morgan and Jess were still in the middle of the same poker game. Katy wasn't sure how long it would take them to get away. She decided to leave before she was obligated to order another glass of whiskey.

The fear she'd felt before had subsided, she realized as she walked away from the bar.

In the darkness behind the bank all was quiet. Laughter and tin keyed piano music could still be heard from the street on the other side. Four men and Katy walked silently to the back door of the bank, pieces of cloth covering most of their faces just in case they stumbled across anyone. Morgan had drawn the short straw to bring the horses around.

Rick was the designated lock picker it seemed. He approached the door first and within seconds had the door open for the rest to enter. They stood crowded just inside door of the bank allowing their eyes to adjust to the darkness. Jess had given strict orders that no one was to light a match under any circumstances.

Feeling movement before she saw it, Katy felt the group shifting further into the bank before she heard Jess's hoarse whisper. "Katy, come guide us."

Katy shuffled to the front of the group and, with bravery she didn't know she possessed, led the men to the wall vault. She stopped at the door and froze. Jess and Rick moved up to the lock. Using their bodies to shield the light, Jess lit a match for only a few seconds while Rick quickly undid the lock. The door was opened and the light was out before Katy had time to realize what they were doing.

"Katy see if you can find the keys to the security boxes. Pete help her." Jess directed as the rest entered the closet and started stuffing money in their sacks they'd hid in their shirts.

The drawers in the wooden desk were heavy and laden with papers and who knew what else. At first she was afraid of touching a spider or a mouse, but after the first two drawers had been pilfered through and realizing Jess and the other were nearly done, she started plundering one drawer after another looking for the keys. Pete had stepped up beside her and was making a more methodical search through the drawers she'd already searched.

As she pulled out the last drawer to search, she felt a sinking feeling in her stomach. What if the keys weren't in here? What if Mr. Franklin still had them on him? What would Jess do then? She carefully put her hands into the drawer, feeling around the papers for any sign of the keys. Sliding the drawer back in, she stood up empty handed. Pete continued his search, while Katy stood there staring blankly into the dark, her mind racing.

"They're not here," Pete called to Jess in the darkness. The men from the wall vault had just come out.

Katy heard Jess mutter a curse into the darkness. "Let's just go. We got enough to make this trip profitable." Katy didn't hear the door to the vault shut as much as she felt the change in the air circulating around her.

They quietly exited the bank. Rick poked his head out into the alley way first. Seeing nothing, he signaled Morgan for the horses. The bags with money were stuffed into saddlebags. The gang dispersed casually as if they hadn't a care in the world. Katy and Jess rode north. Morgan and Clay went east, and Pete and Rick went west.

Only when they were at the edge of town did Katy release the breath she hadn't realized she was holding.

"What's the matter? Nervous?" Jess asked quietly. The steady clop of horse hooves made her fears seem unfounded.

"Maybe." She was nervous. More nervous than she had been for anything in her whole life, but she was with Jess, her protector, so she knew nothing would go wrong. It hadn't so far. Why would it now?

"You're doin' fine. Jus' relax. We'll be home in a few days and when word of this robbery dies down, me and you goin' to have ourselves a good time. What'dya say?"

Katy smiled. "Sure Jess. That sounds nice." She tried to let herself enjoy the quiet night ride as they left town, but her heart deceived her and every little noise spooked her. She imagined the thundering hooves of a posse coming after them with every snap of a branch under her mounts feet.

Hours later they stopped to make camp near a trickling stream. Katy thought it was well after midnight, but couldn't be sure. They spread their bedrolls out without lighting a fire.

Katy was just about to crawl into her bedroll when she heard horse hooves approaching. She tensed and glanced at Jess. He looked alert not tense.

A minute later two familiar figures appeared in the moonlight, Rick and Pete. Katy let herself relax again. She wasn't sure she would be able to sleep, but the rush of the day's excitement had worn off, leaving her dead exhausted and frightened. The two men dismounted and walked up to Jess. In the silence, Katy caught fragments of their conversation.

"See anything out there?" Jess asked them.

"Nah, so far looks quiet." Rick told him.

"I wouldn't hang around too long though. They'll have the Rangers out here after us before long." Pete advised.

"How she holdin' up?" Rick asked tipping his head toward Katy.

She didn't hear Jess reply as the wind shifted and carried his voice away. She saw Rick's head nod in affirmation of his answer, but the constant scowl never left his face.

Despite her doubts and fears, Katy fell asleep quickly.

"Rex what are you doin' here?" She asked. Her brother stood before her with his don't-give-me-any-nonsense face. She sat up from the ground where she lay. She was all alone. The others had abandoned her.

"How did you find me? Where are the others?" She was starting to panic as his expression darkened. The tin star pinned to his chest reflected the sunlight.

"Don't worry about them. What have you been doin' Katy?"

"I've been tryin' to make a better life for myself. We were on our way home with some money that we made. Life will be easier for me now. I don't have to work the fields or mend fences, or the barn or anything like that now. Join us and you can take it easy too." She pleaded with him to understand.

"You know better than that. I can't do that. What you did was wrong. Those people didn't deserve to have their money stolen. They work jus' as hard as you did and I do. Come home Katy, come back and life will sort itself out." His blue eyes flashed. She should've known that would be his answer. He didn't have a crooked bone in his body and was always looking out for the less fortunate.

"Rex you don't understand. Life for me will be the same. No money. No future. No home. I have a husband who cares for me and now I have money to use for leisure."

"Does he really care? Where is he now? Does he really care? Where is he now?" The words echoed over and over again.

As the grey light of dawn greeted the horizon, Katy woke with a start and looked around frantically for Jess. The doubt of Rex's words plaguing her. Five other bedrolls scattered around camp were full of bodies. The other two must've come in silently while she'd slept. Jess was near her. She realized she'd only dreamed Rex's presence. A chill ran down her spine in the coolness of the morning, or maybe it was that her dream had been so vivid.

Taking a minute to collect herself, Katy then sat up and started to pack her bedroll. The sun was coming up. They'd be back on the trail soon.

"Are you scared?" Jess asked as he placed his hands on her shoulders facing him. He studied her face. She was but what he probably saw was remnants of her night full of dreams. She could feel the strain that pulled at her eyes.

With a little difficulty she met his eyes. "Not much."

"Is somethin' else troublin' you?" Katy couldn't bring herself to tell him about her dreams. He would probably tell her she was being irrational and silly. She shrugged.

"Not really." His brown eyes that used to be so warm bored into her now debating the truth of her words. He finally seemed to accept what she said and left to tend to his horse.

Just before the sun broke the eastern horizon, the men gathered with their sacks from the burglary the night before and emptied it on a bedroll. Katy's eyes went wide. She'd never seen so much cash in one place before.

Jess quickly took over and started dividing it up. She noticed only five stacks of money and that Jess was taking double. The first tiny seed of greed began to grow in her. Was half of that hers that he was keeping since they were together? Would he give it to her later to spend for herself or would he spend it for her? She wasn't really good with figures, especially money. She'd never had or seen much of it to learn. Each man, with the exception of Jess, walked away with what she counted as a little over a thousand dollars apiece.

Each man quickly stashed his pay, mounted, and rode off in seemingly different directions. They were on their own. They were no longer a cohesive group. It was every man for himself. Jess pocketed the wad of cash he now possessed and turned to her.

"Ready?"

She contemplated asking him if she was allowed to keep any money for herself, but decided against it. After all she only had to ask and he would give her what she wanted. Or at least that's what he'd told her before.

"Ready." They mounted their horses and headed north.

CHAPTER 11

"You actually drank whiskey?" Rex was incredulous, so much so he fought back a laugh. It wasn't a laughing matter, but he did wonder at how she'd walked out of the saloon. For a such a small girl who'd never had a drop in her life before then, it was a picture he couldn't quite get.

"Yeah," her mouth cocked in a half smile, but quickly left, "and it wouldn't be the last. Change started happenin' rapidly from there, and it wasn't the good kind either. I was at war with myself. I'd committed my first real crime and I paid for it in so many ways." Katy shuddered, her eyes no longer focused. Rex felt her falling into a dark hole, one he was afraid she needed help to get out of. He wrapped his arm around her shoulders, hoping having him there would keep her from falling too far into the dark chasm.

A log popped on the fire creating a small spray of sparks. The room was warm and cozy. Darkness had descended hours ago leaving only the light from the fireplace and a small candle. Jess and Katy were seated together watching the fire. Katy felt safe and secure.

Their journey back from Texas had gone smoothly despite her misgivings. The initial thrill and excitement were wearing off. Katy absently wondered how soon the next outing would be, if Jess would ever take her to a preacher to be properly married, what Ma and Rex were doing, if they still worried over her or not. Overall she was becoming comfortable in her new life.

"When the search for us dies down would you like for me to buy you some pearls or diamonds to wear around your neck?" Jess asked. His warm breath tickled her just before his lips brushed the curve of her neck. The tingling sensation she felt when he was like this created the butterflies in her stomach that always came with his kisses.

"I'd like that." Katy answered breathlessly and surrendered herself to him like she always did. She'd long ago dropped the pretense of a future marriage and took life as if they were bound by law. After all this was uncivilized territory.

"I have some business to take care of. I won't be back today." Jess told Katy as she walked into the house with her pail of milk from the day.

Over the last several days Katy had noticed Jess getting more and more restless. He was probably preparing to start planning the next robbery.

"Can I come with? I'm sure I could help." Katy pleaded, not liking the prospect of staying there alone.

"No." His reply was sharp. Maybe even a little too sharp. She was about to beg him to take her with when she saw the look in his eye. She couldn't explain it, but something told her to leave it rest. After all it was only one night. What could possibly happen? Her and Ma had spent weeks and months alone, granted she had known her neighbors the voice of doubt told her. Here she knew virtually no one. Here she didn't know the land or the people. She was in a foreign country for all the familiarities she had. He walked out the door without another word.

Trotting horse hooves brought her back from her thoughts, the pail of milk dangling in her hand. The walls seemed to close in, the atmosphere was suddenly quiet, and fear seemed to take shapes of its own. She tried to push the shadows from her mind as she went through her daily routine.

She tried cheering herself thinking of the jewels Jess might bring back from his journey. An hour after he'd left she'd checked to see if he'd taken the money from its hiding place and he had. After she'd discovered its absence she'd been skeptical, but had quickly talked herself away from the doubts. He'd come back with something for her, she just knew it. Maybe tomorrow she would go see how Ginny was doing, especially after being absent from her uncle during the heist. It might cheer them both up.

Shadows were stretching long, and darkness had almost completely claimed the land when she heard the steady plod of a horse. Jess was coming home early! She wouldn't have to stay alone after all.

Jumping from the chair she sat in, she threw her sewing supplies aside, and raced out the door. She stopped short. It wasn't Jess who sat astride the horse a few yards from the house. It was Clay. All of Katy's fears seemed to leap from the shadows at once. A shiver ran through her.

"Good evenin' Katy." Clay greeted with a smile. "Don't look so sad to see me, although I'm sure I'm not the one you were expectin'."

"Good evenin' Clay. What do you want?" The forced politeness was the best front she had. He seemed very smug and sure of himself as he dismounted his horse, tied it to the rail and walked up to her.

"Jess, will be here soon." It sounded weak even to herself but she was trying to buy herself time as Clay approached her, the look in his eye anything but innocent.

"We playin' that game? Or do you really not know?" He asked, his cold blue eyes dropping down to her breasts before coming back up slowly. She started to step backwards into the house, but realized she'd only be trapped.

Fear held her thoughts in a vice like grip. "What are you talkin' about?" What didn't she know? What game was he talking about? Had he seen Jess? Had the Indians taken him? Was he murdered and dumped somewhere out on the trail and Clay had passed by him?

"Your innocence makes you much more attractive than what I'm used to." His arms snaked around her waist. She tried to gently push him away and not let panic over take her. "How you ever ended up here, I'm not sure I'll ever quite understand."

He leaned into her, a faint scent of whiskey on his breath. She leaned further back continuing to push against him, but was quickly realizing the more she pushed, the tighter he held her. Maybe she was doing this all wrong. She stopped resisting.

"What do you want with me?" Her voice sounded braver than she felt.

"Surely you don't have to ask." He leaned in and pressed his lips hard against hers. She cried out in pain, but it was muffled by Clay's mouth. She'd hoped by giving in he'd loosen his hold on her, but her anguish only seemed to spur him on.

"Clay please don't." She managed to escape his crushing force for a second. He was breathing heavily now. His hold on her hadn't lessened.

"Why not? You know you want me just as bad as I want you."

Somehow she knew denial at this point would not help. Panic was rising as her mind was in too much shock to find a way out. "Clay you know this isn't right. Jess will be mad when he finds out."

"Why do you keep callin' him Jess anyway? His name is Will Whitaker. Besides how's he gonna find out huh? You gonna tell him? I'll tell him you invited me, but he won't care anyhow. He's got other opportunities he's attendin'." His fingers worked at the buttons on her shirt. She tried to push him away, her mind in full blown panic. The words he spoke barely penetrated. He stopped trying to undo the buttons and pulled the two sides apart sending buttons flying everywhere.

A scream pierced the cool air. Katy heard it before she realized she was hearing herself. Clay pressed himself against her, crushing her mouth with his as he ripped further through her undergarments. She wanted to scream again only this time for help, but knew it was no use. No one was near enough to hear her.

Pushing her into the house, Clay stripped her completely. The savagery that he came at her with numbed her mind. When he was finally finished with her, he'd left just as quietly as he'd come.

Her shivering body finally woke her mind enough to wrap in a blanket, but even the warmth of the blanket couldn't stop her shaking. She had no tears left. She tried to close her eyes and blot it all out, but her mind's eye replayed the scene before her. Jess would be home soon she told herself over and over, but the long lonely hours of the night stretched on.

In the fading light of the fire, she spied Jess's bottle of whiskey he kept on hand for whatever purposes he chose. She remembered the courage it'd given her the night of the burglary. Maybe it would give her courage now. She knew men passed out stone cold drunk too. Maybe if she drank enough of it she could sleep and not relive the events of the evening, again, in her mind.

Fire burned down her throat as she turned up the bottle with a shaky hand. This time the burn was welcome. It took her mind away from what she'd endured. For a few seconds.

What would she tell Jess? Could she tell him anything? Clay seemed to think he could convince him it was her idea. Who would Jess really believe? Surely he'd believe her; after all she was his wife. Well sort of.

She took another swig out of the bottle. Her mind was no longer numb, but was reeling so fast it was stumbling over itself. She sat down in the middle of the floor. What had Clay said about Jess's name? Her unfocused mind struggled to remember, but couldn't. It couldn't have really mattered or she'd have remembered it.

Another job was in the making, she knew it without being told straight out. How could she face Clay again? Would he laugh at her and tell the others what a cry baby she'd been? Would he tell them she invited him over? Would the others come for her too? A shiver ran up her spine at the thought. She took another deep swig of the whiskey. It didn't burn so much now. The shivering had stopped.

What if she became with child? Would Jess be able to tell it wasn't his? What would he do to her if he found out? Would he leave her? Again the whiskey came to her lips.

It didn't matter. She couldn't change a thing now. Maybe she could move out further west. No one would know. She could start a new life. Maybe find a way to get her share of the money from their heist and disappear forever. The bottle kissed her lips again.

She felt numb again, but this time it was a different kind of numb. This time there was no pain, no fear. Now she could face the morning light. Well, maybe after another sip. She took another swig enjoying the feeling of nothingness. Yes, this is what she needed. Nothing. Nothing at all. No feeling. No pain. No doubts.

One more she told herself. It was magic life-giving liquid in a bottle. She took a drink and set the bottle beside her. She lay back on the floor, looked up at the ceiling for a second, and promptly passed out.

CHAPTER 12

Red flashed before his eyes as murder suddenly seemed the most logical thing to do. Rex ground his teeth to the point that looking back later he'd be surprised he hadn't cracked any. He didn't trust himself to speak at first.

"Is Clay still part of the gang? Do you know where he lives?" Katy's head snapped up at Rex's deadly voice. Rage flowed from every pore of his body. She wanted to sink into his strong arms that were wrapped around her and disappear from the world. Her protector was finally here, if not a bit too late.

"Yes and yes. Will you take him into Fort Smith if you catch him?"

"Yup. Judge Parker will be happy to make a date for him with a noose when he hears his crimes."

"Does that mean I have to come to court and talk?" A stark fear spread across her face.

Rex realized what that would mean for her. It was humiliating, but what choice was there? He reached for her hand with his free hand and squeezed it.

"Don't worry. We'll figure it out, together."

"If I talk then the others will be in trouble for their part of the robberies too. They're not all bad and now that Jess is dead there's no one to lead them. They'll scatter to the wind."

Rex gave a querulous look. Was she protecting somebody? Why?

Light filtered through heavily lidded eyes. A hammer was pounding through her skull. She blinked. She blinked again. Light poured into her eyes and the hammer in her head felt like it was busting through. She slammed her eyes shut. The hard surface beneath her felt strange. The wooden floor. Bits of the night before started flitting across her fuzzy mind.

Jess. Jess was due home. It was light outside. She couldn't be seen like this. She opened her eyes, squinting. She felt like screaming at the hammer in her head, but her tongue felt like cotton. It would do no good. She tried to stand on her feet, but wavered unsteadily before sinking back to her knees. The room spun. She pressed her eyes closed trying to make it stop,

She started slowly this time. Finally she managed to balance on her feet. She looked down at her near nakedness. She was starting to feel cold.

She needed clothes, a drink, and a fire. A chill swept down her neck. She hurriedly got dressed and started working on the fire. The drink could wait until the chills that were gradually growing stopped threatening to make her shiver.

The sun was already tipping west by the time she'd managed to drink enough water to stop chewing cotton. The chills had ceased and she was almost feeling human again. She'd managed to milk the cow, and get through her other daily duties. That's when it started. Faint images of the night before started flitting across her mind. Squeezing her eyes shut she tried to push them out, but they didn't go away. More came back. Every time a flash of memory from the night before came back she'd tell herself Jess was coming home anytime, anytime she'd have a protector to hide behind.

Shadows darkened and stretched their arms. Jess was still not home. Katy found herself at a window or the door almost constantly. If he didn't hurry it would be dark again, and she'd be alone. Alone with her nightmares.

Dinner was waiting, the smells teasing her cramping stomach, begging it to eat. She hadn't dared eat a bite all day after it started rolling as she moved around the small cabin. Now the tantalizing smells of potatoes and onions wet her taste buds, a small slice of beef soaked in broth. The minutes stretched into hours and still Jess didn't return. She'd given up pacing and had settled in on the porch, finally letting the fire in the stove go cold. She would light a candle soon to see.

The shadows of the night deepened and started closing in on her. Katy lit her candle and walked inside. She couldn't see into the dark anymore and an eerie feeling of being left alone once again began to haunt her. She tried to eat alone, but the food was cold and tasteless.

She settled in a chair with her previous nights buttonless shirt and tried to repair it. She told herself the shirt could be fixed. She could be fixed. If she just got the shirt fixed up she could forget everything and things would be fine.

By the second button her fingers were having trouble aiming at the right place. The third button was worse. Her hands shook with fear as her mind came to life bringing more of the horrors from the night before, the cold eyes watching her every move, the sound of buttons popping off her shirt and scattering across the floor, the sound of her own screams, the manic smile that creased Clay's face. Katy gave up working on the buttons and set the sewing aside. Why wasn't Jess home? Did his business dealings take him longer than he'd thought? Had something happened to him? She remembered Clay's words. What had he meant?

Another thought began to form. What if Clay knew something had happened to Jess? What if Clay came back again tonight knowing Jess wasn't coming back? Doubt assailed her until she thought she would go mad. She looked around the cabin desperately for something to take her mind off her train of thought. The cabin was spotless, thanks to her tireless work and boredom most days.

That's when she spied it. The thick glass reflected off the low candle light. Like a siren it called to her. Courage and oblivion awaited. She turned away. What would Jess say when he came home and found her drinking? She could see his look of shock and horror just thinking about it. She walked away. She paced. Fear had taken root and was steadily growing. It was too dark to go look for him on the road somewhere, besides she didn't even know where to begin. Why didn't he come? She asked herself for the thousandth time. She paced.

It'd been dark for hours when she gave up on Jess coming home. She was tired. Changing into her night clothes, she crawled into an empty bed. She lay there on the edges of sleep. Every time she would drop off into sleep she relived the previous night. With a jerk and beads of sweat on her forehead, she'd wake up again and again. She couldn't take it anymore. By the fading embers of light cast by the fire almost burned out, Katy got out of bed and retrieved the whiskey bottle.

Taking a swig, and then stoking the fire, she settled into a hard, straight backed chair in front of the fire place. She stared into the fire, watching the flames dance, as she sipped off the bottle, letting the burning in her mouth and stomach burn out the memory and fear.

With a soft clank the bottle slipped the last inch from her slack fingers to the floor as soft, fearless snoring sounds came from Katy's limp body draped precariously over the wooden chair. She barely twitched the rest of the night.

The next morning Katy awoke feeling stiff and sore from her distorted position. Forcing movement into her tingling limbs, she started her day and hoped Jess would return before another night of terror.

The familiar sound of hoof beats sounded outside. Katy held her breath almost afraid to look out the window. Afraid Clay was returning for a repeat, she held her breath. The day was barely half over but she didn't even think daylight would keep him away if he was a mind to come.

Peeking out the corner of the window, she saw the familiar form that was so dear to her. Jess was home. She flew out the door on light feet. A familiar self confident smile crossed his face as he saw Katy running to him.

"Miss me?" He asked dismounting.

Collapsing in his arms she was afraid to speak, afraid the cask of tears that had been boiling all day would burst all over again, afraid she'd tell her terrible secret and suffer the consequences. She just nodded her head as she buried into his shoulder, letting his embrace absorb some of the fear from her bones. She was safe now. No more nightmares.

After a minute of standing there, bare foot in the packed dirt, Jess picked up her chin with his fingers and kissed her. Tears pooled in her eyes as relief continued to flood her. She blinked them away. For a brief second she thought he tasted different today, a peculiar smell she didn't recognize, but then forgot about it just as quickly.

The stars were twinkling brightly with barely a cloud in the sky to blot out the moon. The days had shortened so much that sometimes it seemed they were gone in a blink of an eye. Katy was relaxed now that Jess was home again. The night didn't seem so terrifying now. She stood over the stove cooking their dinner humming softly to herself.

Jess ambled in to the kitchen and headed to the shelf where he kept his ever present bottle of whiskey. Katy caught his movements out of the corner of her eyes and automatically stopped humming, pausing as she waited to see what would happen, if he'd notice. He picked up the bottle, took a couple steps, and then paused. His expression darkened. He held the bottle up and shook it.

"Do you know somethin' 'bout this Katy?" Jess's voice was low and menacing.

The moment of truth was here. She turned to face him, her eyes pleaded with him for understanding.

"I-it was me, Jess. I-I.." The words wouldn't come out as he closed the distance between them in one long stride. His eyes went nearly black as anger washed over him. She could feel it, but when the huge calloused hand came at her time froze and lasted an eternity. The next thing she knew she was on the floor. Stunned and speechless she stared up at him. Salty pools formed in the corner of her eyes. Her happiness lay shattered on the floor around her like broken glass.

"What were you thinkin'!" He raged. "What's possessed you woman? You act like you ain't ever been alone 'fore. You act like some senseless prairie chicken. You want whiskey? I'll get you whiskey, but you keep your pretty little paws off mine!"

"I-I'm sorry Jess. I w-was scared." Her voice quavered and shook. She stayed on the floor afraid to move. Afraid of what he'd do to her next.

"You're pathetic. If you can't handle stayin' here alone when I'm gone, maybe you should find somewhere else to go." Her face paled. Where would she go? She couldn't go home to Ma now. Things would work out. She knew they would. They had to. She didn't have any choices left.

Jess stalked from the room brooding and silent. On unsteady legs, Katy stood and finished the cooking.

CHAPTER 13

"The next few weeks were a blur. We readied for another foray. This time it was goin' to be in Kansas. Jess figured with the cattle being driven up that way it should be a good market. It was a mistake, a terrible, terrible mistake." Katy shivered as the events of that expedition flashed before her mind's eye.

Rex squeezed her reassuringly, hoping she wouldn't freeze up now. He was still having trouble wrapping his mind around the things she'd been through and what she'd done already.

The cool wind lifted wisps of her blonde hair, tossing it here and there, as they rode. Katy tried to crawl further into her new heavy jacket Jess had bought her last week. As always when they travelled she wore men's clothes. The jacket was just as manly as the rest of her look, even the fading yellowish purple ring below her right eye where Jess had slapped her when he'd discovered she'd drank over half of his whiskey bottle while he was gone, gave her a more manly look.

Unconsciously, she brought her hand up to touch her eye as she thought about that night. The following few days had passed in silence between them. Things had a way of working themselves out and life returned to normal. She acted like nothing happened. He never apologized or gave excuses for his anger. She'd just have to learn how to avoid making him angry.

Turning her gaze to the barren landscape, devoid of color and seemingly lifeless, she pondered how much her soul looked the same. The light breeze sent a chill down her spine. A sense of foreboding seemed to hang in the air. She closed her eyes. It's just your nerves, she told herself. You've done it once, you can do it again.

Glancing at Jess's confident form astride his black horse gave her the slightest bit of confidence. He'd been planning this foray almost since they'd returned from the last. He knew what he was doing. It would go just as smoothly.

Tucked away in a quiet hotel room, not far over the border from the Territories in Kansas, Katy donned what she'd come to think of as her disguise. With the layers of blue skirts pinned and tucked, she felt like a real lady, not a bank robber. She glanced at her reflection in the small mirror above the wash basin. An unfamiliar face peered back at her. It wasn't the content and happy reflection she remembered from before. This person looked forlorn and desolate. The bruise beneath her eye was no longer a shadow on her face, but she still felt the ramifications in her heart. The shadow that had descended on it darkened her whole countenance.

Jess lay relaxed on the bed, his eyes closed, resting. He wasn't asleep. She knew better than that. He'd watched her carefully dress and made sure nothing was out of place before he let his eyes close. Her disparaged gaze fell on his ever present whiskey bottle. She needed courage. She needed encouragement. She needed somebody to tell her she had what it took to do this. Confused as to why she would be afraid this time after the last had gone off so easily, she tucked her pistol under the folds of her skirt and tied it securely. The sense of foreboding that had shadowed her thoughts days ago was back clouding her courage. She turned away from the whiskey bottle. She couldn't. It would appear unladylike to have it on her breath at the bank, not to mention she couldn't stand the thought of facing Jess's anger today. It was too risky. He might have her arrested just to spite her. She picked up her small satchel, gave her skirts one more going over, and quietly left the room.

Slipping out the back, the same way she'd come in dressed like a man a few hours earlier, she casually made her way onto the sidewalk of the hard packed street. A chilling wind blew against her, tossing her skirts and her hair in every which direction. What would happen once winter descended on them, she wondered as she walked down the street.

Katy was deep in thought when she almost ran into a man stepping out of the general store. She stopped herself a half step before colliding with him. Looking up, she looked straight into the blue eyes of Pete.

"Excuse me miss." Pete tipped his hat. By the time the words were out of his mouth, his eyes opened wide in recognition. He quickly replaced it with a blank look. Stifling a laugh and trying to appear a stranger, Katy continued toward the bank. That was all the confidence she needed. Her courage returned knowing that she wasn't easily recognizable between the lady she was now and the man she'd be later.

Stepping into the brightly lit bank, Katy walked up to the bored looking teller. His eyes briefly ran the length of her appreciatively.

"I need to speak to the man who can help me with a delicate financial matter." She met his gaze confidently.

"I'm sorry miss, he's out and won't be back until later this evening." Katy frowned. This was not what they had planned. What banker in his right mind left his bank in the hands of a teller?

"What am I to do with my valuables until then sir? I shouldn't have them on me parading them through this lawless town!" The indignation in her voice was nearly genuine as her mind raced ahead.

"I'm sorry miss. He holds the only key for the safe."

"Oh good heavens he doesn't even trust his own employees!" She was working up a rant and could see it was frustrating the teller as red crept into his face at her last remark. "Tell me then, is there another bank in town?"

"No miss." The teller's voice strained as he tried to remain calm.

"Well, I've never heard of anything so ridiculous."

"I'm sorry miss. I believe Mr. Wheeler's mother is on her death bed and he's gone to say his goodbyes. As I said he is to return tonight and will be here first thing in the morning if you would like to come back then."

"It looks as if I have no choice. Good day sir." Katy spun on her heels and stalked out the door leaving the flustered teller staring after her.

Slowing her pace just out of sight of the bank windows, Katy began pondering what their next move would be.

Slipping into the hotel room silently, she found Jess just where she'd left him. The soft click of the latch on the door didn't even disturb him. She set her satchel down and sat on the only chair in the room to remove her shoes.

"What'd you find out?" He didn't even bother moving as he spoke to her. He just laid there with his arm over his eyes.

"Nothin'. Absolutely nothin'." This brought him fully alert. Seeing the look in his eyes made Katy uncomfortable as she rushed to explain. "The teller at the window told me the owner was away but was due back in tonight. He's been gone to be with a sick mother or somethin'. I couldn't get access anywhere and that's all I know. I'm sorry Jess."

Silence descended on the room as Jess's dark eyes grew pensive. Katy unconsciously held her breath, waiting for his tirade that she was sure would follow at her lack of information gathering. She couldn't meet his gaze. Staring at the colorful pattern of the quilt on the bed she couldn't help but to admire the intricate design. She found her eyes roving the walls and really noticing the room for the first time as the silence continued.

"Did you check the train schedule?" The sound of Jess's voice in the quietness of the room nearly made her jump.

"I-I didn't think too. The teller didn't say he was comin' by train." Jess scowled at her.

"Looks like I have to do it myself." He stood and stuffed his hat down hard on his head. His beard and hair had grown out again. She thought he looked dirtier that way, but he told her it was harder to recognize him with hair everywhere. It was true. He wasn't quite the handsome man she'd run off with months ago. Now he looked the outlaw he was as she wondered again what kept her with him as he stomped out the door.

She relaxed into her chair and closed her eyes. This wasn't what she'd hoped and dreamed life would be like when she left home. She wasn't supposed to be a fugitive from the law. Sure it was exciting and all, but when would they leave this life behind and move on to better things. The money they'd taken from the last bank seemed to have already vanished. She didn't have the nerve to come out and ask Jess directly how much was left, but he'd made out like they were short on cash again.

The door silently swept in on its hinges a short while later when Jess returned. She was standing there in only her chemise and corset changing from lady to man when he entered.

"We're still on. There's no way I can contact the rest of the gang before it's too late. The train's not due in till after nine tonight. We'll make sure we're out before then."

The rest of the afternoon passed with each minute seeming like an hour.

"I'll see you at the saloon later." Jess had reached his breaking point just as the long evening shadows descended on them. Katy had begun to wonder if he would wear out his boots or the floor first with his incessant pacing. She hoped he won a few hands at cards before their bank excursion later to make sure he was in a good mood, just in case. The foreboding feeling she'd had all day hadn't lifted. In fact it had only grown into a palpable fear. She wouldn't dare mention it to Jess. He would only laugh at her and call her a silly girl.

Waiting until the sun had completely set and darkness crept into every corner, Katy made her way out the back door of the hotel once again and headed for the rendezvous at the saloon.

The sounds of high pitched laughter, tinny piano music, and the general din of male voices reached Katy long before she reached the swinging doors of Thirsty's Saloon. Taking a deep breath to steady herself, she pushed open the doors to a sight that she was still unaccustomed to. Painted women sat in men's laps laughing and carrying on, men glared at each other over the tops of the cards in their hands, others sloshed back mugs full of foamy beer, and she felt terribly out of place, again.

Finding an empty space at the bar, she stepped up. From her vantage point she found Jess involved in a game of cards, Rick was talking to a raven haired painted woman, and Pete who appeared to be half drunk, sat in a corner nursing a foaming mug of beer. Clay was nowhere to be seen, but she had a pretty good idea where he could be found. After her experience with him, she'd bet money he was upstairs with one of the resident women of the place.

"What'll it be?" The squirrely little bartender asked her. The grey streaks in his hair testified to his age although his stature was that of a younger man.

"Whiskey," Katy said in her deepest voice she could muster. The squirrely little bartender only blinked at her once before scurrying off to get her whiskey. She let out the smallest sigh of relief. She needed courage tonight more than last time. Maybe it was the knowledge of what they'd be doing this time that was her undoing. She wasn't sure. All she knew was that her hand had started to shake before she left the hotel when she was tucking her hair artfully under her hat giving her a shaggy unkempt look. Stealing a glance at Jess when her whiskey appeared, he seemed totally oblivious of her.

The glass of amber liquid called to her like a siren. She sipped at it first until she noticed the bearded cowboy nearest her eyeing her suspiciously. Inhaling quickly she tipped the rest of the glass back in one quick motion. Her eyes all but bulged out and she fought back a cough. The man seated beside her let out a deep rolling laughter. She felt her face grow warm with embarrassment.

"That's it sonny. You're on your way to bein' a real man." The heavy paw of the bearded man clapped her on the back. She was wearing her gun and was tempted to call the man out, but knew she'd be the one laying on the wood floor in the end, not him. She opted for taking it the best she could and let the man have his laugh.

"Let me buy you your next drink." All she could do was nod as he motioned for the bartender to bring her another whiskey. "What's your name boy?"

Name? Name! She couldn't tell the man her real name or he'd be suspicious. She tried not to panic. She couldn't think. She was panicking. "My name is Cade."

Well it wasn't her most brilliant moment, but her voice hadn't shook like she'd feared it would. She genuinely sounded like a youth in his changing years.

"Well Cade, tell me how a youngster like you ends up in a place like this?" The man seemed the talkative sort. Katy knew she'd really have to work on her lying if she was going to survive this.

"I'm jus' passin' through with my uncle."

"Your uncle eh? He's not one of them cattlemen is he?" One of his bushy eyebrows raised in obvious dislike for the breed. The drovers were known to cause the most problems, especially once their cattle had been sold and they'd been paid.

Brushing back bits of straw colored hair from her eyes, she shook her head. "Nah, we jus' pick up odd jobs and travel around."

"No other family? Nowhere to put down roots?" The man's face mellowed as he set his mug on the bar to listen to her story, looking at her with empathy.

"Nah, my folks is dead." She'd deliberately tried to sound indifferent and unattached.

"Sorry to hear that. Least wise you gotchur uncle. Sounds like a decent fellow to string ya along."

"Yeah." She wanted to run from the prying man, but had nowhere to go. Snatching her glass of whiskey off the bar she tipped it back. This time instead of closing her eyes to the taste she quickly looked to the others in a silent plea for help. Jess had his back to her. Rick was staring intently at the dealer across his table. Pete was the only one who seemed to even be remotely reachable and his eyes appeared half closed. She was stuck.

The warmth of the whiskey coursed through her again, warming her blood, and had started building her courage. As she set the glass back on the bar, another body squeezed in between her and the talkative bearded man. Katy glanced over. It was Clay. Her blood went cold. In less than a second she made her face impassive. The bearded man looked somewhat indignant, but after glancing at Clay's pistol he wore, he must've decided against argument.

Clay was looking quite pleased with himself and rather unstable as he grinned at her. Even through the haze of the smoky room, his blue eyes looked hard and ice cold.

"Barkeep, two whiskies." Clay motioned that one was to be for her.

"Thanks, but I'm done." Katy told him, meeting his cold eyes head on. Where'd he come from? Wasn't he supposed to be occupied with one of the women?

"Oh come on now *boy*. A man don't stop drinkin' till he can't walk."

What was he trying to do? He knew they had a job soon and if she was drunk it could risk their whole operation. Did he hope to catch her alone after the robbery?

The whiskey arrived and she tipped it back before the cold shiver could run down her spine at the prospect of another meeting with Clay.

"Come now, that wasn't very friendly. You didn't even wait for me." Clay admonished. Again he motioned the bartender for a drink for her. She glanced around to the bearded stranger hoping he'd distract Clay, but he'd turned to one of the painted women who'd walked up to him and was deep in conversation with her. She was doomed. She just hoped Jess wouldn't beat her for it later. She caught herself just before she involuntarily touched her eye that'd only recently healed from his powerful slap.

A fourth whiskey appeared before her. Its amber liquid dancing in the dim light telling her courage was at the bottom of the glass.

Reaching for her glass, she held it up in salute to her benefactor. Clay smiled like the devil he was, and together they tipped their glasses back, draining every drop of the beautiful liquid.

It was strange, Katy thought, that Clay of all people had almost rescued her from the talkative man, but in turn was getting her drunk, giving her courage. Her hands had ceased their shaking, she felt warm, and her fears were beginning to fade into the haze of the room.

From the corner of her eye she saw Pete stagger drunkenly out the swinging doors into the night. That was the signal it was time.

"I better be goin'. My uncle will be wonderin' what's keepin' me." The bold face lie made Clay look toward the chair Pete had just vacated. It'd been said for the benefit of the bearded man just in case he'd been listening to their conversation.

Clay tipped his hat in acknowledgement of her leaving. She walked out of the saloon on legs she barely felt. The brisk air that greeted her at the door threatened to sober her completely, but the whiskey had settled too far down in her stomach to leave so suddenly.

Making a circuitous route around the streets she took up her position.

CHAPTER 14

"The whole second operation had a bad feelin' from the start. I was beginning to see whiskey as my friend. It gave me the courage I lacked. I even faced Clay again and found that I didn't completely hate him as I probably should. Jess wasn't lookin' out for me anymore. He'd pretty much turned his back on me and I don't think he ever looked back. I had to look out for myself. It was all I could do." Katy's voice was distant as it seemed the events leading her to the point played so vividly before her eyes.

"I was afraid of being left alone. I was afraid of goin' back to Ma. I was afraid of stayin' with Jess with the violence he'd shown me. I was jus' plain afraid of everythin'. What else could I do but follow the path I'd been lead down and hope for the best?"

Rex wanted to comfort her and tell her he'd always be there for her, but the words wouldn't come. What if he wasn't always there for her? What if he couldn't be? What if something happened to him and he failed her? What if he couldn't get her out of the mess she'd gotten herself into? He'd fail her. He couldn't promise her the things she needed to hear the most. He felt his heart squeeze at his helplessness to help her.

The bank was dark, as they'd hoped. It appeared the banker hadn't made it back from his trip yet. She breathed a sigh of relief. They'd left Morgan to watch for the returning banker just in case they'd been wrong about his returning by train. Pete had drawn the straw to hold the horses this time. The other three would be there soon. She just hoped a wondering deputy didn't happen by on his nightly rounds as she leaned against the rough wood of the building a few doors down from the bank in the alley.

It felt like hours, but in actuality it had been maybe twenty minutes before the others appeared. Jess silently led them to the back door of the bank. Rick stepped to the door and worked his magic. The door swung in silently.

Jess and Rick entered, hands resting on the butt of their pistols. Clay slipped in behind them, followed by Katy who wondered if Clay wasn't a little too drunk tonight. He didn't seem as graceful as the others. Morgan came up silently behind Katy, almost making her jump at his unexpected arrival, but remained behind at the door. The train must've already delivered its passengers, without the banker aboard.

It was difficult to maneuver around the bank silently with so little light. The moon was only half full and was hiding behind the clouds, rarely taking a chance to peek out. They were feeling along the walls looking for doors or anything that felt like it might be a safe or a vault. Unfortunately they had no idea what they were looking for exactly, Katy berated herself for not getting any more information to help.

"Over here," Rick's rough whisper came, bringing the scattered gang together to the corner farthest from the door.

A second later Jess lit a match, a flash and sound of Rick's Colt firing almost made Katy scream just before the room was suddenly plunged back into darkness. The four of them seemed to hold a collective breath straining to hear if the shot had brought running footsteps to investigate the sound. Nothing happened.

Katy let her hand fall from holding her racing heart. A moment later a lock slipped from its hinges. She was surprised at the primitiveness of the lock, but didn't have time to think on it further as they slipped as a single shadow into the closet like room.

Again Jess flicked a match on. The shelves where not laden as the last one had been. Katy hoped they weren't robbing an empty bank.

Just then the sound of horse hooves approached. The match was extinguished, plunging the room into darkness once more as everyone froze. The clopping of hooves stopped outside the bank. A soft muttered curse came from Jess's direction.

"Katy. Window." Jess ordered.

Her feet felt like lead. She'd been the closest to the door. Now she tried to walk silently to the shade drawn windows. What she saw made her heart sink and even the whiskey couldn't chase away her fear now.

A portly man was removing a small carrying case from the seat of a buggy directly in front of the bank.

"The banker's here!" She whispered as loudly as she dared. A shuffling of feet told her the others were on the move. She fled after them, her heart racing.

A lock clicked on the front door just as Katy reached the back door. She swung the door behind her too quickly and it made a slamming sound in the silence. Wincing when she heard a man's voice on the other side say "what the devil," she looked up to see Pete racing into the alley way leading their horses.

They were all fleeing on foot down the alleyway to meet Pete and their horse's when the back door opened. She found she was slower than the other men as Pete held her chestnut colored mare's reigns out to her when the banker shouted down the alley.

"Sheriff! Sheriff! I've been robbed!" The man yelled over the clatter of the hooves as they attempted to flee into the night.

Ducking low on her mount in case the man had a gun he wished to start shooting at them, Katy raced after the others as they fled down the back streets heading for the edge of town. She was trailed only by half a length to Pete, at least that's who she thought was so close behind her. In the darkness and terror of it, she wasn't really sure.

A muzzle flash and the report of a shot came from in front of her as they raced down the back street, the banker's voice still shouting for the law. Another flash and a shot came from somewhere to the right as they fled. Katy ducked her face into the flying mane and held on for dear life. She was armed but there was no way she was letting one hand go of the horse at this pace.

More shots erupted as the galloping hooves sounded down the street, and more shouts erupted. She hoped her horse followed the rest, because at the moment she was too terrified to lift her head and see where she was going.

After what felt like hours, the shots faded into the background, the only sound was of two horses galloping. Realizing she wasn't fully alone, she risked a glance back. The other horse had slowed, but only to avoid the flying feet of her mount. The rider hunched over and looked to be bobbing somewhat irregularly.

It was then she realized the other horse was gaining on her again, her mare was slowing seeing the excitement was over.

"Keep goin." The hoarse voice sounded like Pete. It also sounded pained.

Katy matched pace with Pete's horse. "Are you hit?"

"Don't worry, keep goin'." Katy looked ahead for the others, but they'd all disappeared, more than likely scattered in every direction of the wind. Cuss words jumped to her lips, but she bit them back before she could utter them. Jess had finally deserted her.

A stifled groan came from Pete. She looked over at him again. He was injured and trying to hide it. He needed medical attention and they were on the run from the law. Suddenly, she felt vulnerable and helpless as they raced into the open darkness of night.

A few minutes later Katy realized her mare was starting to sound a little winded, she pulled her in. It didn't sound like they were being immediately pursued. Pete's horse slowed with hers, which was good because she didn't think he was capable of doing much with the animal at this point.

Another groan came from Pete as his horse slowed. He hadn't lost complete consciousness yet. Reaching for the other horse's loose reins she guided both mounts into the nearby woods. The clouds were moving on. The sliver of moon provided just enough light to keep the horses from tripping as they slunk along in the shadows.

Pete had inched down across his horse, yet somehow he managed to remain in the saddle.

"Pete. Pete." Katy called to him, hoping he'd respond showing her he wasn't unconscious. He didn't. What are we doing to do? She thought. By now the law was probably closing in on them. With

Pete unconscious they couldn't go much further. Where was Jess? Rick? Clay? Morgan even? How'd they all disappeared? Every path her mind travelled ended up with her in jail. It could be worse right? She could be dead after that shoot out. She shivered at the thought. She was stone cold sober now. To top it off, the temperatures were dropping.

A dark shadow formed to the right further into the treeline. She turned their horses toward it, hoping it was a good enough shelter till morning when she could actually see where they were going. Approaching the dense wood, she saw it might even be better than she'd hoped. A fallen tree and a mess of vines provided a natural shelter from the sight of the road.

Walking the horses behind their shield, Katy dismounted. She left an unconscious Pete on his horse as she cleared a place for him to lie. How she was going to get him there was the next feat. Forming a hurried, makeshift bed of fallen leaves, she returned for Pete's horse's reigns. She walked the horse up as close as she could.

"Pete." She tried again. No response. He was almost twice her size. Reaching up she untangled his hands from the reigns. He leaned further over toward her. She shook her head wondering what she was doing. Grabbing him under his arms she pulled him toward her, at the same moment his horse took a step forward. He slid from the saddle, knocking her over and landing on top of her with the sudden shift of weight. He moaned as they landed on the leaves in a crumbled heap.

The ungraceful landing knocked the wind from her for a split second. Rolling Pete off her, she wriggled out from under him. He was built solidly. Muscles built from hard work, felt firm under her touch. It struck her then that he wasn't a bad looking man; in fact he was actually quite good looking. What was she thinking? Was she still drunk?

Drawing her mind off her train of thought, she returned to the horses. She couldn't tend to his wounds yet because she couldn't risk a light to see where he was injured. Unsaddling both horses, her mind went to work on how to see the wound that rendered Pete unconscious. It had to be bad. Would he die? The thought stuck her like a hammer. She couldn't put it off any longer she had to work on his wound.

Using the blankets from under the saddles she hung them on branches, enclosing their camp the best she could. She lit a long match and searched Pete's body starting from his head to check for injuries. When she reached his shirt it was soaked in blood. She couldn't work with only one hand. It was time to light a small fire. If the smoke drew the posse, at least he'd get the medical attention he badly needed.

Working quickly, Katy had a small fire going close by under the shelter of their make shift camp. A chill swept her as the fire came to life. She hadn't worn her jacket. She only hoped it was in her saddle bag still. Turning to Pete, she ripped his shirt off. Again she was distracted by the form of his muscled body. She stopped her fingers before they ran down his chiseled chest.

Fresh blood was coming from a hole on his left side. Some had already dried. Was it the entrance or exit hole? Pushing him onto his side took nearly all her strength, only her years of working the farm had built enough strength to move this man around. A smaller bullet hole entered at the back slightly diagonal from the wound in the front. The bullet had gone through and not lodged inside of him. That was good. He might have a chance to survive.

Shredding his bloodied shirt into strips, she wrapped his wound hoping the bleeding would stop. She felt his skin. It was still warm to her touch, but under it were chills. Fever was setting in already. In the unfamiliar area she had no idea where there might be water. She felt helpless and frustrated. How was she going to keep Pete alive?

While the fire still burned, Katy searched both their saddle bags for blankets, shirts, anything to use to keep him warm during the long hours of the night ahead. She found her jacket Jess had given her and an extra shirt in his bag. She wrapped him in both, trying to keep his movement to a minimum without a thought for herself, she wouldn't be doing much sleeping anyway.

After she'd done what she could for Pete, she extinguished the fire. She hadn't heard a sound in a long time. Maybe they were safely tucked away in the woods. Or maybe the posse was waiting for first light to come after them and take them to jail. Was attempted robbery a hanging offense? Katy stared at the dark sky wondering what would happen come sun up.

CHAPTER 15

"Did Pete die or is he the one you're protectin'?" Rex finally broke the long silence to ask.

"Why is it that things happen at the wrong time?" Deliberately side stepping the question, Katy turned pain filled eyes to Rex. "Nothin' ever goes like you think or hope it will. My whole life I've always been one step too late."

"It's not too late now, Katy. There's still hope for you. You can still have a good life." Rex said softly, but all she did was shake her head. He realized how empty his words sounded even to him. He didn't have a right to call justice for the law even with his own sister.

What was he going to do? He couldn't see her spending years in the dark shadows of the jail. Finally, he settled for sitting there in silence, waiting for her to continue her story. He was in no hurry to take her back where a dimly lit cell awaited. The stench of the jail made even the sturdiest of men queasy.

The darkness of night wore on and the fever took firm hold of Pete and held him in its clutches. He tossed and moaned throughout the night. Curled up next to the fallen tree, Katy tried to block it out with her hands over her ears, but somehow the sounds seeped through. She was helpless till morning.

Goosebumps prickled her flesh as the wind began to howl and moan through the trees. Her sheltered place behind the blankets was no longer enough to keep her warm. Her teeth began to chatter uncontrollably. Getting up and moving around didn't help either. Every time a shadow moved she ducked down, afraid of being seen. Most of the time it was only an owl or a cloud passing over head, but her nerves were on edge and her good sense had left hours... no weeks before.

Placing her hand on Pete in a moment of his silence she felt burning skin, yet the cold bumps were still present on him. The only way either of them were going to survive without being half frozen to death was body heat. The horses had wondered deeper into the trees, searching for food and shelter from the wind. Katy took down one of the horse blankets that reeked of horse and sweat, and placed it over Pete. He began thrashing around in his fevered state.

Leaving the other blanket up to block the wind from directly hitting them, she curled up beneath a corner of the blanket covering Pete, turning her back to him. Too much of the chilling wind crept in still. She turned toward him, tentatively placing a hand on his chest. His restlessness stilled.

Sleep didn't come easy to her. It came and went at will. Pete was surprisingly restful, so much so that at times Katy would startle herself awake afraid he was no longer breathing when he hadn't made a sound or movement for a while.

Grey light finally crept over the horizon. Feeling somewhat relieved, but bone weary exhausted, Katy rose from her position on the ground next to Pete. It was time to do something, but what she wasn't sure. She didn't dare risk a fire yet. Her stomach growled in protest to the emptiness it felt after so little sleep and her foray with whiskey the night before. How near to a house were they? Water? Anything? Did she dare leave Pete in his state to venture out to look for anything?

Before the sun completely topped the horizon and a posse had time to form, she needed to do something. There wasn't much time left.

In the growing light she took in her surroundings. There was a road on one side and dense woods on the other. Now what? Where were the horses? She walked the short distance to the edge of the woods. The horses weren't near the road. She turned and walked deeper in to the woods.

What if the horses wondered off and someone found them before she did? What if the posse found them and were somehow able to identify them as ones used in the attempted robbery the night before? They'd be getting company very soon.

Deeper into the woods Katy went, hoping the horses were still nearby.

After walking for several minutes she spotted a brown shadow half hidden by a tree. Was it a deer? Were the bears still out foraging or were they already in hibernation? Her tired eyes tried playing tricks on her every time she blinked and tried to bring into focus what animal was standing behind the tree.

Finally realizing it was one of the horses, she felt a small wave of relief wash over her. She was almost completely beside herself when she realized the horse was drinking out of a small stream of cold clear water.

Hurrying back to camp she found a canteen. Pete had started thrashing around in his fever again. She would need to check his bandage when she returned with the water.

After returning with water, Katy dug through the saddlebags once more in search of more material for bandages. The shirt that wrapped him now was crusted with blood where more had seeped out after she'd wrapped him during the night. It was then she remembered she still wore her chemise under her man's shirt and the binding that kept her womanly figure from showing in her disguise.

Unbuttoning her shirt she unwound the binding from her chest and removed her chemise. Stooping beside Pete, with her shirt again buttoned, she gently unwrapped his wound. As she peeled off the last layer, a small stream of blood began to run and he moaned. She quickly poured the cold water onto her chemise to wash the dried blood from the sides of his bullet wound. Rolling him to his side again, she washed around the hole in his back. Moving as quickly and gently as she could she used her strip of cloth she'd used for binding to wrap his wound tightly.

The heavy coat Jess had given her was now stained with blood. She briefly wondered if it would wash out later or if she'd have a permanent stain in it from Pete.

The sun cast a warming glow down on their little shelter as the day began to wear on. Katy's stomach had given up growling and now sat pouting like a rock inside of her. Pete's moaning and thrashing didn't help her nerves either.

Katy had considered going out to forage for something to eat, hoping against hope something would turn up, when she thought she heard horses coming down the road. Stilling her movements she strained to listen. That's when Pete began thrashing and trying to talk in his delirium. Panic over took her. If that was a posse coming down the road they would be sure to hear Pete. She looked frantically around for something to quiet him, but nothing came to her. If she used the horse blankets, they were too heavy, she might smother him to death. She couldn't stuff leaves in his mouth to muffle him. She looked back to the road. Three men on horseback were barely visible. Were they within hearing distance? She wasn't sure.

Leaning into Pete's ear she whispered "you gotta be quiet Pete or they'll find us." She felt ridiculous talking to a delirious man who wouldn't be able to know what she said especially when his head rolled back and forth as he tried to speak again.

In a moment born of desperation she pressed her lips to his hoping to at least muffle his moaning and muttering. His lips were cracked and dry, and surprisingly he grew still and silent again. Lifting her head slightly to look at him more closely the pallor of his face was a stark reminder that death lurked near. She felt a strange stirring in her chest again. He needed water, he was dehydrating fast between the fever and the cold wind that had blew all night.

His head rolled again. Fearing he was about to start thrashing about again she leaned back over him with her lips firmly pressed to his. Her heart beat quickened. The three men were almost beyond their hiding place. The present danger was almost gone. She told herself it was the anxiety of almost being found that made her heart race not the kissing of an unconscious man.

She felt silly kissing Pete every time a horse and rider passed on the road, but it worked. They made it to dusk without being discovered and somehow Pete was still alive.

Every time Pete would start his delirium Katy would sit on the ground, put his head in her lap, and try to dribble water into his mouth. She needed broth for him, no, she amended her thoughts, she needed to get him to a doctor but that was out of the question. It was too dangerous, besides she didn't have a clue how she'd move him. She slammed the canteen down on the ground in frustration. Looking at the shadows playing across Pete's face she knew what she had to do.

CHAPTER 16

"Tell me Katy, what happened to Pete? Did he die on you?" Rex's soft voice probed, trying to break down the barrier walls that surrounded his sister.

Her lips twitched as if she tried to smile. "Not in the sense you're talkin', but there's nothin' to be done about it now."

Rex's eyebrows came together as he studied his sister with a hard look. "Care to explain?"

After a moment's hesitation Katy's blonde hair moved softly in affirmation.

Darkness was falling quickly. Katy waited patiently for the moon to come out, maybe it was nervousness as going out alone to do what she had to, or maybe it was fear of leaving Pete alone in his state, defenseless and near death. Her empty stomach knotted tighter. She'd pulled both horse blankets over Pete, knowing he'd probably throw them off before she returned.

The moon spilled light across the landscape making the way easier as Katy rode at a slow trot toward... hope? Survival? What was she riding for anyway? Maybe she should turn around and try to find her way back to town and turn herself and Pete in? They didn't hang people for trying to rob a place, did they? No, that was a useless idea. What would she do when she got out of jail finally? Jess surely wouldn't take her back. She couldn't return home? She'd end up a woman of questionable repute. She'd heard the stories of deserted women in Fort Smith. No family, no money, nowhere to go, they all ended up the same way.

Lost in thought, time became obscure. Dark outlines appeared as the hills gently rose and fell. Cow? Yes, those were cows grazing. The first wave of relief washed over her, but just as quickly a new knot formed in her belly. Would a bullet kill her immediately? Or would she be forced to suffer and languish away as Pete was doing even now? She slid off her horse and tied it to a fence rail. She'd have to go on foot from here.

The house was closer then she'd expected. Pausing behind a scrawny, scraggly tree, Katy studied the layout. Soft light drifted out from only one window back in the corner. Whoever was still up she hoped was preoccupied with something inside. A smaller building sat off behind the house.

That must be the store house. The barn was closest to her.

On feet that felt made of rock, she ran behind the barn. Stopping to catch her breath and to listen for shouts or gun fire, she steadied herself. The cool air stung her lungs and helped keep her alert.

From the corner of the barn she peeked around the side. The light from the lone window could barely be seen. She let out the breath she'd been holding and ran to the store house. Quietly she turned the latch. Hoping a wind wouldn't come up and blow the door shut she stepped inside. Closing her eyes for a few seconds she opened them again letting the lack of light adjust her eyes to the shadows.

Moving slowly as to not disturb anything, she felt around for something she could easily carry. Finding two small slabs of dried meat she quickly exited the structure. As soon as the door was shut securely, she bolted towards the edge of the field where her horse waited patiently bent over trying to nibble at any patch of grass it could reach.

If she was shot at would she hear it before it tore through her skin, Katy wondered as her heart beat sounded like a stampede in her ears. She was too terrified to look back. Her breath came in long gulping gasps by the time she reached her horse. Ducking behind the fence post she sat down. As her breathing steadied she risked a glance behind her. No running shadows chased her. No shot guns sounded in the chill night air.

Standing on shaky legs she managed to mount her horse. Strange she didn't have a name, Katy thought suddenly as the soft thud of the horse's hooves went back the way they'd came. For all the travels they'd done lately, her horse was nameless.

Clutching the prized meat close to her chest she wondered if she was beginning to lose her mind. She could've just been shot or even killed, and here she was wondering why her horse didn't have a name.

The moon was starting to dip further in the midnight black sky as panic threatened to overtake her. Had she passed their hiding spot? Could she find it in the dark again? Could she find it come light even? Gripping the unknown meat tighter she fought the rising fear in her chest.

She'd passed it. She knew she had. Should she stop here and wait till dawn? Would she be found once daylight came? What about Pete? He couldn't survive without her. There were wolves, his fever, his wound. She had to find him tonight.

Her horse nickered. She froze, legs clamped tightly against the bare horse flesh ready to kick her into a dead out run. An answering nicker came from the tree line. Could it really be? Had her nameless horse just found their hide away? Her horse answered again and nodded it's head in the direction of the other.

A flash of fear passed over her. What if some Indian was lying in wait to scalp her, or worse? Well, she thought, it couldn't be much worse than what Clay had already done. She let her horse have free reign. The mare didn't seem the least bit afraid as she clopped over to the trees.

A murmur of jumbled words came to Katy as she entered the trees. Relief flooded her. She'd made it back to Pete, alive. She wanted to laugh and cry all at the same time. Tumbling off her horse she stumbled to Pete.

"Look," she said holding the two small slabs of meat up, "we have food." She didn't really expect a response from him, but it felt good to say it anyway.

A chill wind began to pick up, making her shiver. The horse blankets that had covered Pete lay askew around him. She wanted to build a fire so badly to let her bones thaw out, but it was too great a risk especially tonight. If the owners of the house discovered their missing meat they could easily find them come morning with the scent of the fire. At least she had food, her stomach growled just thinking about it.

Forcing herself to be civil, she dug for a knife in the saddle bags. She cut small chunks and tried to eat slowly, but soon found herself swallowing half chewed bites of the dried beef. Meat had always been a commodity to her, but this tasted like manna from heaven. Her stomach wrenched into a knot. She stopped chewing and clutched at the pain just before her prized food came back up.

Panting at the violence of the attack, she wiped her mouth and took a drink of the icy water she kept nearby in canteens. She would have to take a different approach. Before long she'd managed to keep a small portion of the dried beef down and lay curled up to Pete as she had before, drawing on his body's fevered heat to keep her warm under the stench of the horse blankets. Her last conscience thought was how long would she have to draw out the meat.

Days and nights became a blur. Exhaustion threatened to overtake her as the cold only slowly sapped her of strength.

As she had every day, she made her trip to the trickling stream deeper in the woods. Today it felt even longer. Pete had been quiet most the night. He would probably die on her today, Katy thought as she trudged back to their camp. She set the canteens downs. She couldn't even bring herself to look at Pete, not now, not when death was so close. A raspy sound startled her. Spinning around she looked into the smoky blue eyes that'd been closed for so long. Cracked dried lips moved making the raspy sound that had caught her attention.

"You're alive!" Katy fell to her knees and kissed the all too familiar cracked lips. As she realized what she'd done she drew back quickly embarrassed.

"Water." Came the hoarse whisper, as the blue eyes seemed to study her somewhat confused.

Grabbing the canteen of fresh water, Katy lifted Pete's head as she tried to help him drink. Icy water trickled down the light brown growth of his face and dripped on her arms. He tried to reach up with his hands to hold the canteen and guzzle the water when she took it away.

"Slowly." She spoke softly stroking his hair. His eyes met hers again. As she realized what she was doing, she stopped. She'd become so accustomed to his unconsciousness and being there that she felt she knew him on a far more personal level than he did.

"Where... where are we?" His hoarse voice rasped out. He continued to stare at her like he was trying to make sense of it all.

"I'm not sure really. After we left town with the others we got separated from them. You must've rode slower because of your injury. When the shooting stopped and I finally looked up you were the only one around. I don't know which direction we rode or where we are. I think we've been here five days. Maybe four I'm not really sure."

"Why?" His eyes fluttered, she wasn't sure if it was pain or if he was slipping back into unconsciousness again.

"Don't worry 'bout it. Rest now. We'll talk again later. I'm not goin' anywhere." She watched as his eyes closed again. His head rolled to the side as his body went limp.

Tears pulled at her eyes as she turned away in case he awoke again. She didn't think she was capable of crying anymore, but now she let the tears make trails that threatened to freeze on her cheeks. After a few minutes of giving in, she straightened her shoulders. It was time.

CHAPTER 17

"Three days later I helped Pete onto the back of his horse. It was slow goin' since we had to stop often to keep him from passin' out and fallin' off his horse, but he got us pointed in the right direction."

A smile almost creased Katy's lips as she thought back. "After the first couple days of travel we started stoppin' at houses and askin' for the barest of nourishment or shelter with the story that Pete was my brother and somethin' had spooked his horse causin' his injury. By then I'd stolen a clean shirt for him. His wound was slowly healing. It was a risk we took, but it was well worth it. After several days of real food and warmer sleeping conditions, Pete regained his strength faster, and we were able to travel further."

Rex kept his silence. This wasn't the sister he'd left in Fort Smith. The woman seated next to him now was practically a stranger, a strong, scared, harmless stranger.

Rough hewn logs appeared through the trees. They'd made it back! Finally. Katy wanted to jump off her horse and run through the front door to Jess's waiting arms. It'd been such a long, hard trip she thought she might fall to pieces right there staring at her home. Glancing over at Pete, who's only sign of injury was a tense jaw she'd learn to recognize as hiding pain, he sat quietly on his horse.

Words suddenly felt hollow and meaningless. Here sat the man that had sheltered, protected, and guided her back home. Now she felt a strange sense of betrayal as she slid off her horse to go to Jess.

Goodbye seemed to catch in her throat. Silently Katy began to unbridle her horse to let her rest after their hard journey.

"I need to talk to Whitey if he's home." Pete's soft voice carried in the silence. The hoarse raspiness left by the fever and dehydration had almost completely disappeared from his speech.

"I'll get him for you." Katy offered knowing that it was still difficult for Pete to mount and dismount his horse. The paleness left by his lack of blood and fever still seemed evident to her under his scruff covering his face. He had tried to shave it twice on their trip, but couldn't stand to hold his arms up long enough to do the job. She'd offered to do it for him, but he'd refused.

Hanging the bridle on a nail near the door, Katy walked into her little cabin. It felt cold. Had Jess not kept a fire going? Wasn't he freezing?

"Jess. Jess, I'm home." Katy called into the cabin. It wasn't like there were many walls to separate them. In the half minute that it took to peek through each door, she realized he wasn't there. She stood there perplexed. Where was he?

Walking back outside, she faced Pete. From his reaction she must've still looked puzzled.

"He's not here. Maybe he's out huntin'." Katy suggested, but the dark look that crossed Pete's face made her think he doubted her words.

"I'll go look for him and if I see him I'll let him know you're back, safe." Before she could respond to him, he'd jerked the reigns and rode off.

As she watched Pete's straight back ride away, she felt a peculiar pain in her chest as if something was being ripped out. She shook her head, childish imaginings. All other thoughts of Pete, she mentally pushed out of her head as she began building a fire. Jess would be home soon and he would come running to her happy she was home and safe.

It no longer matter why they'd been separated after the failed robbery. They could still carve out a life for themselves. Maybe now Jess would see they should move farther west, maybe to the gold fields and stake a claim there. A change of scenery would be nice. They were wanted criminals now, surely it wasn't safe to stay here.

After starting a fire and finding some food, Katy glanced out the window for the hundredth time since her return home hoping to see Jess's familiar silhouette coming from the trees. The horizon was still empty. Shadows grew longer as her hope began to dim. Pete hadn't found Jess. She would end up spending a lonely night in their cabin alone, again.

In her desperate flight back, she'd almost forgotten her nightmares at home, but as the long shadows turned quickly to night she began to fight back chills that were more than the cold night air. Catching herself pacing, she'd rub the chills on her arms, then try to sit down and sew. In less than two minutes the needles would be sitting frozen midair as her mind wondered again and she'd renew her pacing.

After what felt like hours, she broke her resolve and went in search for Jess's ever present bottle of whiskey. Taking a long sip of the bottle, she welcomed the fiery liquid as it seared its way into her belly. Since they'd left Kansas, she'd not had a sip. There'd been no need. Now in the house full of nightmares, whiskey was her only escape.

Sipping on the bottle, the night wore on and still Jess didn't return. With a numb mind, limbs, and heart, Katy stretched out on the empty bed, the bottle of whiskey close at hand. She stared into the pitch black ceiling asking herself why she'd returned here. No welcoming arms had reached for her. No words of relief or happiness had greeted her on her arrival. Instead, she lay in the darkness trying to block out the nightmares of her life.

The next morning dark clouds hung in the air, wind whistled its chilling warning that nasty weather was on its way. Through foggy eyes and a mouth full of cotton Katy returned to her normal routines hoping that the rest of her life would return to normalcy as well.

As reason returned and her head cleared, a new fear began to grow in her stomach. Had Jess been arrested and was sitting in jail somewhere? Did she dare go looking for him? What would she do if she found him? Were any of the others still free, or had they all been locked up? Maybe she should try to get to Morgan before the weather started in. He would know if Jess had been arrested and if all of them had been she would need to check on Ginny. The poor girl needed a better life than what her wayward uncle could give her.

Glancing at the skies again, Katy decided that if she was going to see Morgan and find out if her fears were justified, she needed to go now or get caught in whatever the skies decided to hurl at her today.

A figure approached on horseback from the west as Katy mounted her mare, turning her toward the trail. Stopping the horse to watch the lone rider, she all but held her breath. She'd heard stories from Rex about lone deputies riding up and arresting people before they knew what was happening. A knot of fear formed a rock in her stomach. That was it. Jess was locked away somewhere and the law was here to take her to be with him. What would jail be like? Should she run? No, if the law had tracked her this far, they could find her anywhere, besides where would she go? She couldn't possibly make it back to Fort Smith without help. The rest of the gang was likely in jail beside Jess, the only one that might still be free was Pete and he was injured.

As the figure came out of the shadows, her shoulders sagged in relief. It was Jess. She turned her mare around, spurring her into a run toward Jess. A huge smile lit her face.

"Jess! I'm so glad you're here!" Katy pulled up reigns as they met. All she could think about was jumping from her horse and throwing her arms around him. She needed to draw from his strength. He stayed in his saddle.

"You made it home finally I see." His cold words made her almost physically jerk back from him as if he'd slapped her face. Icy wind whipped at her face. Her mind was no longer blurry, the hard edge of Jess's words hung in the air as she struggled with his indifference.

"I was so scared. I was jus' headed to see if Morgan knew where you were. I was afraid you might've been arrested and locked in jail, but you're here! I'm so glad." She felt like a small child trying to explain how they'd broken a dish on accident.

"I'm not in jail and don't intend to be. Let's get inside before it starts rainin' on us. I'm cold enough as it is." He was mad at her, she could see it in the set of his jaw and hear it in his voice. Was it because she hadn't been able to keep up the night of their escape? She was baffled at his response to her.

They quickly unsaddled their mounts and as they crossed the threshold of the cabin, sleet began to fall, sounding like flat notes tinkling across the leaves. Katy didn't take the time to shed her coat, but wrapped her arms around Jess as soon as he stopped in front of her. She wanted to cry, she wanted to laugh, she had a hundred questions for him, but right now she needed to feel his arms around her. But he stood without moving.

Stepping back she looked up at him in the dim light. His eyes were cold and hard. She had to find a way to make them thaw.

"What took you so long gettin' back? I thought I told you to keep up when we left town?"

"I… we.." words seemed to get lost in her throat as she tried to explain. There was so much to tell him that it all got tangled on her tongue.

"So you admit that you were with Pete?" Katy paused. Had Pete found Jess and told him about their flight?

"Did Pete find you then?"

"He found me, but I want to hear your version." There was no warmth in his words. They were accusations that were as sharp as the icy wind that howled past the windows.

"When we fled from town, I tried to keep up, but I was so scared, I barely looked to see where we were going. The horse seemed to know to follow you, but when I finally looked up I didn't see anyone. Only Pete was behind me and he'd been shot. That's probably the only reason he was there, otherwise I'd have been completely alone."

His eyes darkened as she rushed on to explain how she'd hidden them in the woods and barely survived. She left out the parts about sharing the horse blankets with him, and how she'd acted when he was talking out of his mind. No one but her knew those things, and she was the only one who needed to know.

"When we finally got back yesterday you weren't here. I was so afraid you'd been caught and taken to jail. Pete left right away, said he might see you, and tell you I was home."

"What did the two of you do while you were alone?"

Katy's face blanched. Did he really think something improper had happened? What had Pete told him? Had he told Jess something had occurred between them? What kind of woman did he think she was?

"Nothin' happened. What did he tell you happened?" She stammered.

A pain seared across her cheek before she saw the movement coming. "He told me the same story that's why I think yer lyin'! You whore. Tell me what really happened!"

His face was inches from hers. How could he think they were both lying when they'd both told him the same thing? Her cold fingers touched her face fighting back the tears as she touched her flaming cheek.

"That's what really happened. Nothin'. I'm with you. I wouldn't be with anyone else as long as you have me." Blinking hard against the tears, her voice cracked as she pleaded with him to see the truth.

"I don't believe you. You were alone for weeks. You can't tell me nothin' happened." A fist flew from his side and landed solidly in her stomach. She cried out as she doubled over. "That should take care of any bastard growin' inside of you," he said as he turned and walked away from her.

Laying there in the floor she couldn't keep back the dam any more. She let the tears spill into tiny puddle on the floor. Her body hurt. Her heart hurt. Why couldn't Jess see she'd had no choice but to come back with Pete, and nothing had happened? What had she done to make him doubt her?

Less than a minute later he returned from the kitchen, glowering over her. "Where's my whiskey woman?"

With red rimmed eyes she looked up at the man who was becoming a stranger to her. Fear filled her again. She'd forgotten to put his bottle in its place.

"It's next to the bed." A foot flashed out and kicked her back. The shooting pain made her cry out again.

"I told you not to drink my whiskey! You dirty whore. Get your own damn bottle and leave mine alone." With that he stalked into the bedroom after his bottle. Fresh tears streamed from her face. Her happiness lay shattered around her. She couldn't move.

It felt like hours that she'd lay there on the cold floor, but it couldn't have been, for when she finally found the strength to get up Jess still sat on the bed, and there was still whiskey in his bottle.

Not daring to speak to him until his dark mood had passed, she crept around as quietly as she could the rest of the day trying to show him she could still be a good wife despite his misgivings about her. She would have to be careful not to anger him again and be the image of perfection if she didn't want any more beatings. With the dead of winter upon them she wasn't sure she could make it until another successful robbery improved his mood.

CHAPTER 18

A blank expression filled Katy's eyes. Rex sat there in silence wishing he'd been the one to have killed Jess for what he'd done to his sister because right now his blood was boiling and he was itching for a fight. He had the sudden urge to go beat Jess's lifeless body, although he knew it held no relief since Jess wouldn't feel the pain. Damn the cowardly bastard that beat his sister! What had she been thinking to stay with him?

He studied her face. The tears from before had left muddy trails on her cheeks. The blank expression haunted him. There was no sign of the former girl he knew. This was someone completely different. This wasn't his giggling sister he'd heard outside the barn dreaming of her prince charming. This was a beaten and broken woman whose sole future rested in his hands.

Maybe he should resign from his position and the two of them could disappear into Mexico or even Canada? No, that wouldn't work. There was still Ma to think about and other women like her who needed his help to escape their pathetic lives.

Had she told him anything that would help keep her out of prison? She'd willingly gone along on their robberies. She'd not been forced into anything as far as the gang's activities were concerned, so what was he going to do?

With a deep breath to calm his boiling blood he turned to her again. "What did you do all winter?"

"Nothin' really. We mostly stayed inside the cabin. Jess would leave for a few days at a time on occasion, but always left me with my own bottle of whiskey, especially after that beating. I think he knew that was the only way I could cope. Only I started drinking it even when he was home, it helped passed the time and made me forget the things he'd done. He didn't beat me as often or as bad as the time I came back from the foiled robbery with Pete. He even talked nice to me and treated me like his wife most the time, but by the end of February I could tell he was ready to get back to business." Katy's voice was hollow as she spoke. The life and feeling she'd once expressed so openly was gone. There was nothing for her now.

"I've got a new plan boys. We're goin' to start a new business this year." Jess spoke with excitement to his men that were gathered around the rough wood hewn table in the kitchen. It was the first time the group had gathered as a whole since their last excursion that had gone sour. Katy stood behind and to the side of Jess allowing her to watch all their faces. Most of them looked eager, only Morgan and Pete listened with any sign of trepidation.

"We're goin' to start collectin' our pay from stagecoaches." All eyes came alert at his words. Only last night had Jess told Katy of this new venture he'd been carefully considering and planning. "I've been readin' about how others are doin' it. I think we can do it better and get better pay outs than hittin' the banks like we were."

"Don't you think it's a bigger risk? Most stage drivers carry some kind of rifle or shotgun and you don't know who's riding along." Morgan queried. Katy had also expressed similar concerns to him last night.

"I didn't say it'd be easier, but at least we'll know our targets. It won't be hard to disarm one driver and once the driver complies the passengers usually lose their courage to resist. Easy pickings. Besides that way we won't have a whole town or a sheriff and posse on our trail straight away. Gives us more time to melt into the countryside undetected. Are you with me?" Jess's eyes were shining. Katy didn't have to see them to know. She heard it in his voice.

A few unsettled looks passed around the room before heads began nodding. It looked like they were going to take their leader's words for it despite any personal doubts they had.

Sitting diagonally across from her, Pete caught her looking at him. He seemed to have recovered. His eyes flicked across her body before they held her gaze for a few seconds. She felt a blush rising in her cheeks as she took in his freshly shaven face that exposed his lips, making her wonder how it would feel to kiss him without the fever. He was a good looking man. His whipcord muscles she knew lie under his shirt made her think about things she shouldn't. He'd been one of the few who'd treated her like a woman since she'd left home. She looked away. If Jess caught her look she was sure he would read what thoughts crossed her mind. He might even beat her here in front of all his men.

Jess was still talking, explaining his next plans. She hoped he hadn't seen the look that had passed between them. Pete's face was unreadable, but Katy was sure hers was as plain as day what she was thinking. What would Pete think of her wondering thoughts? Would he think she was nothing more than a whore like Jess had accused her of? She hoped not. He was one of the only people whose opinions of her mattered, and she wasn't even sure why it did.

The men dispersed before Katy had collected her thoughts completely. Jess appeared before her making her focus on reality.

"I'm leavin' for a few days. Try not to drink the whole jug of whiskey while I'm gone." He tipped her chin up and kissed her hard as if reminding her of his claim on her. Then he was gone. Katy sank into a chair. In a way, the times when he left were such a relief. She didn't worry about being beaten.

She knew he wasn't in jail, and he'd be back just as sure as the trees grew tall. She didn't really know where he went, or what he was doing since all the men had just left, but she assumed it had something to do with their plans for their stagecoach business. Clay hadn't been back since the first time he'd stopped by, but that incident was never far from her mind when she was alone.

By the time shadows began stretching long across the yard, Katy had finished her usual chores. She'd just picked up her needle when she heard something outside. A horse? A cold chill raced down her spine as images of the night Clay visited came vividly into her mind. She ran to the shadow of the window and peeked out as she held her breath.

A rider was coming up to the house. Pete? She stepped out where she had a better view. What was he doing here? Had he forgot to tell Jess something before he'd left? Katy went to greet him.

"Hello Pete. Jess isn't here. He left for a few days." Katy said as Pete reigned in his horse.

He dismounted without saying a word. "I didn't come lookin' for Whitey." He stood only a few feet away from her. He looked at her with pity, almost like he didn't know what to say. What was going on?

"I know he isn't here. That's why I came. I saw his horse earlier while I was comin' back from my grandpa's. I don't know how to say this…" Curiosity piqued her interest. What wasn't he telling her and why? He took a deep breath like he was about to deliver bad news. "Do you know where Whitey goes when he leaves?"

"I have no idea. I figure he's gatherin' information for the next set up."

Pete looked down at his feet, studying his boots like he could change their color just by staring.

"What is it Pete? What are you tryin' to tell me?" The silence that was engulfing them was wrecking havoc on her nerves. She could picture all kinds of horrid things if she left her imagination dwell on it.

"Whitey is with Pale Moon." He paused as he let his words sink it. "I don't know what he sees in that woman or why he can't be happy with you. You deserve better than him. I don't know what's kept you with him this long."

The words he was saying finally sank in. She stepped back as her hands flew to her chest.

"No. No, you're lyin'. Why are you tellin' me this? How could you do such a thing?" She turned to run back into the house so he couldn't tell her any more, but Pete's reflexes were faster than her. He caught her arm and turned her around.

"All of us know it. She's been his mistress since long before you came along. We were all surprised when he came back with you. For a few weeks we even thought he had changed and really fallen for you, but it didn't take long for that woman to find him in her bed again. I just wish it didn't have to happen to you. You seem like a good person. You saved my life. I jus' wanted to tell you that if I can ever help you, whether it be leavin' Whitey, or whatever I'm here for you."

Katy didn't hear half of what he said. She was still in shock, pain. Her heart was ripping apart even worse than when Jess beat her. Another woman? As she let it sink in it all began to make sense. All the pieces fell into place. A cry of agony swept her being. She couldn't move, couldn't breathe, she just cried.

"I'm sorry Katy. I just thought you should know. I feel like I'm lyin' to you by not tellin' you what's goin' on." His fingers brushed against her hair in soothing strokes.

Any control she'd held onto in front of him suddenly broke. She buried her face in her hands. How had she not known? How did she not see that's what he was doing? She felt stupid for being so gullible. What did he really want from her anyway? As she stood there wrestling her doubts and emotions she felt strong arms around her, as she was pulled against a hard chest.

When the tide of emotions had finally drained her, she looked up into Pete's face. She felt silly. She looked away again.

"I'm... I'm sorry. I soaked your coat." Katy sniffed as she dug out her kerchief from her pockets. The cold air made the tears feel like ice.

A smile cracked his solid features. "It's not every day you get a pretty lady cryin' on you."

His smile was infectious. She felt her lips tugging her cheeks into a half grin. "Would you like to come in and warm up with some coffee?"

"Sure." He followed her into the cabin. She poked the hot coals in the stove and fire place trying to unleash as much warmth as she could find since her heart had been doused with ice.

With red rimmed eyes Katy held her coffee and stared into the glowing fire. Pete sat in the hard wooden chair next to her allowing her the silence she obviously needed to sort the confusion and anger out in her heart. After what felt like hours, Katy glanced at Pete. There was no condemnation, or judgment in his eyes.

His warm blue eyes seemed to give her strength as she held his gaze, before letting her eyes drop to his lips. She caught herself wondering again how they would feel now that they weren't cracked, broken by fever, and their lives weren't hanging in balance over their heads. Looking down into her cup, she hoped he hadn't noticed her roving eyes. Besides who'd want a scarlet woman now that she and Jess had lived together as man and wife without the proper authority.

"Katy, I..." She looked up from her cup as Pete paused as if unsure of the right words. "Can I have some more coffee?"

He ran his fingers through his hair and stood to hand her his cup. She stepped up to him, as she reached for the cup their fingers touched. Without thinking she looked up into his eyes that were so warm and inviting. She froze. Pete didn't relinquish his cup as he stepped closer, making it to where there were barely inches between them. At first she forgot to breathe. Her heart raced wondering what he was thinking, but knowing he couldn't be feeling the same thing as she.

As the seconds seemed to stand still he lowered his lips to her, he finally released the cup as he pulled her to his body. She returned his gentle kiss with a little more persuasion, all of the emotion of the last few months flowing through her, freeing herself as she got lost in his kiss.

"I might be crazy, but you feel so familiar." Pete said in a husky voice when they'd finally broken their kiss

A smile tugged at the corner of Katy's mouth. "There's somethin' I should tell you." He quirked an eyebrow at her, waiting for her to continue. The look on his face made him look so devilishly handsome that she had to look away for a minute and get her wild emotions under control before she spoke. She told him about how delirious he was and about the people, possibly posse's, that came by. "I finally ran out of options, I couldn't think of anythin' that I could do that wouldn't smother you so I kissed you to keep you quiet."

A deep laughter rumbled out of him. the effect his laugh had on her was scandalous.

"Well then I thank you again for savin' my life. Tell me how did I react when you kissed me?"

"You went quiet and still like you knew there was danger all of a sudden."

His hand reached to touch her face. She flinched involuntarily, but caught herself before she pulled completely away. His smile vanished and his look darkened when he saw what she did.

"I'm not gonna hurt you."

"I know that." Smiling at him, she hoped he was telling her the truth, and sensing somehow that he was.

"But someone has. Who was it?" Panic filled her eyes. Who was it? Who hadn't it been since she came to this territory? Clay. Jess. If Pete found out what would he do? Clay's menacing warning echoed in her ears. If she told about either, there could end up being some real trouble and somebody could get hurt, no somebody could get killed.

"Was it Whitey?" He pinned her with his gaze, both hands rested on her shoulders. She remained still and silent. "Was it someone else?"

"No, no, no." She shook her head violently trying to shake the voices of Clay and Jess's threats out of her head.

"Katy look at me." He spoke sternly. With hesitation she looked up. "Let me help you. I won't let anyone hurt you. Besides I don't know why you stay with Whitey anyhow. He doesn't know how to treat women. He jus' uses them." His voice had gone hard.

"If he heard you say any of that he'd kill you, kill both of us probably." Tears pricked the back of her eyes, but she blinked them away.

"He's not a killer. He's mostly all talk."

"You don't know him like I do." Katy looked down. Pete pulled her back to him and just held her. For the first time since she'd left home she felt at peace, but she knew it wouldn't last long. Jess would come home and the cycle would start all over again. She'd already thought about running away, even with Pete it was no use. Jess would hunt them down and kill them, if anything just to spite her. It didn't matter if Jess treated her poorly or not she was his and there was no escape.

"Promise me one thing." He said and waited until she nodded against his chest. "Know that I'm always here for you. If you ever decide you can leave him I'll help you get away. I can tell you're scared of him. I think he's the one who's hurt you too. I owe you my life so the least I can do is try to help you be happy in yours."

Katy fought a lump in her throat as a single tears slipped out. Thank you was all she could choke out when she finally was able to speak.

CHAPTER 19

"Why didn't you let him help you escape?" Rex asked.

"Don't you see? It didn't matter if Jess really cared about me or not, he would've found me and killed me along with anybody that was with me. I was just his property. He made that very clear on more than one occasion."

Rex shook his head. He was disgusted with the whole mess. "What about Pete? He's a fugitive from the law now too."

"I know, but he's never intentionally hurt anybody. He's only helped in small ways with the robberies."

"If the description of him that you gave me is accurate then he was one of the ones holding a gun on me when the stage was held up."

"He only did that because Jess would've kicked him out if he hadn't, besides he wouldn't have shot to kill."

Not about to argue with his overwrought sister, he just raised his eye brows at her. Her answer was a scowl. He'd just have to wait for her to convince him otherwise it appeared.

Three days later Jess came back. The raw emotion she'd felt the night she'd found out about Pale Moon was gone and the only thing she felt now was disgust. The whiskey she'd drank the following two nights had helped dull her pain and senses, but the memory still lingered.

When it came down to it she'd let her mind drift back to the night Pete had came and stayed with her. They'd only risked one night knowing Jess could return without notice, but knowing that one night would be safe. She'd drank until she passed out. Not even his presence could chase away the darkness in her soul. Pete had sat there with her, a silent, comforting shoulder through the darkest hours of night. It was those few precious memories that kept her sober in the daylight hours now as she faced Jess day after day as they prepared for their first stage coach robbery.

The first job they'd decided on would be a place they picked out north of Fort Gibson along the Texas Road. The working reason behind it being that the fort didn't have the resources to chase them, but would have a coach full of possibilities.

Sunlight streamed through the window, making Katy squint her eyes at its brightness. The fog in her head and the cotton in her mouth from another long night made her want to bury under the blanket and just skip the day entirely. The thrill of the robbery was gone after her near escape from the last bank job. The dazzle of a life full of riches and nice things no longer held its appeal.

As she felt Jess shift in the bed beside her, she again asked herself what was keeping her here. Did she really have no place to go? But she knew the answer. Jess had more than made it clear that she was his property and if she ever went against him, or left him, there would be hell to pay. Repressing a groan of utter resignation, she pushed the blanket aside and forced herself to get out of bed, despite the pounding in her head. She had no desire to be near the man that had chained her to the life she now led.

Within the hour, the rest of the gang had assembled at their cabin. It was the first time Katy had seen Pete since their night together under this same roof. Trying to portray an air of normality, she kept her eyes averted and kept quiet as usual. She was glad they stayed for only a few minutes. Once they got on the trail, she could drag the rear and no one would say a word.

Feeling eyes on her back, she risked a glance as she swung her right foot over, she caught Pete watching. Their eyes met for a moment. Katy felt the spark between them, but looked away before she gave herself away. If Jess caught even a hint of anything between them, his volatile tempter would ignite, and they'd both be dead within minutes.

The day was long in the saddle, but the weather held promise. Dragging the rear alone, Katy almost wanted to smile. Spring was her favorite time of the year. Everything was in bloom, the green of the vegetation was so vibrant, even the air smelled like promise.

She missed the fancy clothes she normally got to wear. This time she looked like the rest. Hat pulled low, men's pants and shirt, boots, and her hair carefully hidden. She no longer felt like a woman, but rather a pawn in a chess game, a valuable piece of property to be handled and put to good use. The thoughts were too depressing and she pushed them away, focusing on what was in front of her instead.

Watching the men riding ahead of her, she started thinking how different they all were. They were all rough and hardened, but she knew at least two of them weren't quite as evil as the rest. Staring at Morgan's back she wondered how Ginny was faring. She'd been so wrapped up in her own problems that she hadn't been to see the little girl since the onset of winter.

And then there was Pete. She looked at his rigged figure riding closest to her. Oh the dreams and wishes she could spend on him, but what good would it do her? All the wishing and dreaming in the world wouldn't make it so. The only way there'd ever be a chance was if Jess was gone and by gone he'd have to be dead. Then he couldn't change his mind, he couldn't hunt them, he would not pose any kind of threat whatsoever. The way her life seemed to go these days though the only hope she had was that she'd die quickly by a stray bullet during one the their robberies.

Sighing inaudibly, her shoulders slumped at reality. Watching Clay and Rick ride side by side she felt as if there was an invisible evil force brewing ahead of her. It was almost as if she could reach out and touch it. A shiver went up her spine at the thought of spending time in their company the next few days. With that realization, the vibrancy of spring and lush vegetation suddenly dulled, the coolness of the breeze prickled the hairs on her neck. There wouldn't be much sleep on this trip.

The next day, they passed Fort Gibson close to noon. A few hours later and they were laying their trap. Katy's job was simple; stay back and hold the horses. In the hour before the stage arrived, only one lone horseman had passed unmolested by the gang. After he'd passed, Katy wondered if only a lone rider stood a better chance out there than a passel of people. A group was far more profitable than a loner; however, they could also prove more dangerous.

A plume of dust on the horizon was her first indication the stage was approaching. Until now she'd been calm and lethargic. Hands tightened on the reins of her horse as the normal jolt of adrenaline hit her. Maybe it was her lucky day and the driver would shoot Jess when the men lined up on the road. Pushing the thought aside, she watched as the five men came out of hiding and took their positions in the middle of the road. With faces covered, hats pulled down low, guns pointed directly at the stage, as the jangle of harness's and thunder of horse hooves shook the air, the men stood quietly and calmly.

From her hiding place in the brush, Katy watched the scene unfold. Jess held the middle position an arm's length ahead of the others. Without a word the stage driver reigned in the racing horses. The coach was still a ways out from the men. The driver glanced around. What if he turned the stage around and ran back to the fort? Would they give chase or would they abandon the job? She held her breath without conscious thought.

Jess had seen the driver trying to make a quick decision but he acted faster. He called out over the road.

"Don't even think about runnin'. We can still shoot you or your horses." The driver froze as he realized he was still within shooting range.

Without taking his eyes of the driver, Jess and the rest walked quickly up to the stage. They were too far away from the horses to make a fast get away if any of the passengers decided to get happy with their guns. Katy led the horse through the under growth to a closer vantage point as quietly as she could. There was no point in attracting attention to herself.

Voices floated on the air, but the words were indistinguishable. Watching as the driver and then passengers disembarked from the stage, she could envision the words spoken. Jess stood back with his rifle trained on the group lined up, backs to the stage. Pete passed down baggage to Morgan while

Clay and Rick took up a collection from the passengers. Within minutes, the sacks they'd brought to collect in were sagging with an assortment of things from money to jewelry or whatever had struck their fancy. The passenger's bags lay gaping open while the contents lay strewn across the dusty road.

Kicking her mount forward into a trot while leading the other horses, Katy met the gang. Jess was covering the rear walking backward while the other four ran to meet her. By the time Jess mounted his horse, the others were kicking up dust heading south. Spurring her mare to keep up, she listened for the sound of bullets to go whizzing past her ears.

After what felt like an eternity, but in reality had only been a few short minutes, the gang had slowed and were walking their horses to appear casual to any passerby's. Trying to get control of her shaky breathing, Katy allowed her horse to slow to the pace the others had set. Glancing over her shoulder for the hundredth time, she told herself they'd made it. From here they'd slowly and quietly melt into the brush.

They rode late into the night, putting as much distance as possible between them and the hold up. No fires were allowed when they finally did stop to catch a few hours sleep before they mounted back up the next day.

The next morning, Katy was up at the crack of dawn wondering why they'd even bothered to stop for sleep. All she'd done was toss and turn most the night, jumping at every sound thinking they'd been tracked down. She knew the horses needed the rest. It was still a full day's ride back to the cabin.

The last rays of the sun painted the dark sky the last fading colors of the day as Katy lit the lamp in the kitchen. Gathering around the table each man dumped his sack of loot he'd gathered. She was struck by the odd assortment of things that littered the surface. Cash, coins, jewelry and a small assortment of trinkets among which was a ladies fan trimmed in lace which had come from Clay's sack. Jess too eyed it for a second longer than the rest before he looked at Clay.

"A fan?"

"For Ma. She's always wanted one and we never had anything so fancy 'fore." Clay looked slightly embarrassed at his admission.

Nodding his consent, Jess allowed Clay to keep the fan. The rest he quickly divided amongst the rest, as he kept two shares for himself, presumably holding Katy's portion of the loot with his. Somehow she knew she'd never put her hands on any of it.

A light reflection caught her eye as Jess slipped a particularly sparkly necklace into his pant pocket. A small jolt of jealously struck her as she realized as soon as the men left Jess would leave her to see Pale Moon and give her the trinket.

The other men were stuffing their treasures into pockets or bags, cracking jokes about their fearless adventures. Watching from the shadows, Katy tried to melt into the background and be forgotten. She was counting the minutes until Jess would leave. She was no longer jealous of Pale Moon. All she wanted was an escape. Her feelings for Jess were dead, the motions of everyday were mindless. The only thing she could think of was escape. When the house was quiet and she was alone, she could escape into her whiskey bottle where all her dreams and hopes lay on the bottom.

Quietness greeted her as the sun fell away sending the landscape into darkness. The sound of the last man leaving had reached her just minutes ago. Jess walked in the front door without a word. She sat quietly in her chair near the fire place as she listened to him rummage around their room looking for some unknown object. Soon a fire wouldn't be necessary at night, even now some nights didn't require one. Where would she sit then? Staring into the fire she pondered her future. There was no future. It was something just as dead and cold as the fire place would be in the next month or so.

"I'll be back sometime. I have unfinished business to take care of." Jess said as he walked past her, opening the door, and disappearing into the night.

Katy stifled a sarcastic laugh. Unfinished business? Who was he fooling? Certainly not her anymore.

Walking into the kitchen she retrieved her ever present bottle of whiskey. It was the only thing Jess made sure she had. Uncorking the bottle she tipped it up.

CHAPTER 20

"After I found out about Pale Moon it was easier to deal with the loneliness. I started embracin' that time alone. The whiskey helped dull the pain, but I found out there were other ways to forget the pain of circumstances. It was risky, but I didn't care."

Katy's voice held a hint of disgust, whether at herself or Jess, Rex couldn't be sure. Maybe it was both. Either way he was almost afraid to find out what else she'd endured. He kicked a clod of dirt with his boot. He should've been able to find her before now. He should've ridden to her rescue months ago. She'd been so close. How many times had he passed by within a few short miles?

The bottle froze mid air, tipped up for her second swig of the fiery liquid when a light knock sounded at the door. A drop of the whiskey dribbled out of her mouth as her mind raced. Cursing herself for spilling, she quickly wiped it away and turned to the door.

"Who is it?" Katy called out, her voice sounding stronger than she felt.

"It's me, Pete." Her shoulders sagged at the familiar voice, not realizing how tense she'd really been.

Practically running to the door, she opened it letting Pete glide in quietly. As soon as the door shut, he pulled her into his arms. Almost dropping the bottle as she gazed into his warm blue eyes, she let the spark of his touch run through her. Inches from her lips he paused and looked at her fully.

"Have you been drinkin'?" His face was a mask, but suddenly she felt foolish.

Holding up her bottle she said "Whiskey. It helps me through the nights."

Rough fingers brushed a strand of loose hair away from her eyes as his eyes seemed to reach far beneath her skin, searching for her fears. She thought she saw pity cross his face. Her spine stiffened. She didn't want pity. She wanted escape. With her free hand she reached up behind his neck, stood on her toes, and pulled him to her for the kiss she longed for, the kiss that would make her put the whiskey bottle down and forget about anything else.

When daylight broke the next morning, the brown jug of whiskey still sat where she'd left it the night before near the cabin door. Katy picked it up on her way to the kitchen, tempted to whistle a happy tune, as she swung the bottle with a skip in her step. It was the first time in what felt like years that she could remember sleeping without the nightmares or the haunting shadows crowding her dreams, or waking up without a mouth full of cotton and a head full of soggy cobwebs.

Touching her hair where Pete had gently stroked it until she fell asleep last night, she smiled to herself. There'd been nothing more than those sweet, passionate kisses. It's not that both of them hadn't wanted more, but some invisible thought had been spoken between them that made them understand that Pete had to set himself apart from the other men she'd had in her life, and the only way he was going to do that was to not let either of them give into their primal urges. After he'd sat next to her keeping the darkness out of her mind as she slept, he'd brought one of the chairs into her room and somehow slept in it all night in case she'd needed him. But she'd slept almost as peaceful as a baby, dreaming of fields of flowers and happiness.

Before the sun had come out of hiding from the horizon, he'd kissed her forehead promising to come back if Jess didn't return before nightfall, but he had chores to do at home. It was best he'd left. She had her own work to do. She couldn't spend her time walking around mooning over his blue eyes and strong arms, even if she could almost pretend that Jess didn't exist and her life was here with Pete. With an exasperated sigh she released her hold on the whiskey bottle she'd rested on deep in thought.

Pushing a strand of loose hair back in place she set her hands to work.

The sound of horse hooves met her ears as she placed the last of her lunch dishes into the sink. Had Pete finished early and come for her so soon? The thought was almost too happy to hold its place in her mind. Her stomach sank. No, it was most likely Jess and he was already coming back from his conquest with Pale Moon. With slow steps she walked to the door, prepared to play the part of dutiful wife for all pretenses. With one last sigh she pasted on a smile and opened the door.

It wasn't Jess or Pete. Clay had just dismounted from his horse and was standing there, wrapping the reins of his horse to the rail. When he saw her open the door with a smile, a cold hard smile creased his face and crept into his evil eyes. Swallowing hard, Katy debated her options. This wasn't what she'd expected and was unprepared. She knew she'd have to survive on her own. There was a hunting rifle hanging above the fire place. Could she get to it before Clay grabbed her? This time she wasn't fooled. She could see his intentions clearly written all over his face. The delay she'd managed last time, she knew wouldn't work. They both knew Jess wasn't coming home and there was no one to save her. Her mind raced with scenarios, but her feet felt grounded to the floor.

Menacing blue eyes held her gaze as he casually approached. She felt like a trapped rabbit under the hypnotizing eyes of a snake. When he reached the small porch she finally found her feet and turned to run, trying to slam the door behind her as she flew into the house, heading straight to the fireplace. What was only a short distance felt like miles as Katy ran across the open expanse of the cabin. Eerie, echoing footsteps were coming up behind her.

Two steps away from the fireplace a hand caught her arm whipping her around and making her almost loose her balance.

"Are we playin' games now?" Clay held both her arms in a firm grip as he watched her chest heave more out of fright than exertion.

"No. Let me go!" Twisting trying to free herself from the iron grips on her arms only made him pull her closer. Terror over took her senses and tears began to find their way down her cheeks.

"I don't want to let you go. I like feisty women. Why don't you stop strugglin' and enjoy this as much as I do?" His flat, cold voice froze her in her fight to flee. Instinct told her the more she struggled the worse it would be for her. Could she lull him into thinking she enjoyed him and then escape? Should she tell him Pete was on his way back? She quickly dismissed that idea as it wouldn't have much effect on him and could risk letting Jess find out.

Taking a shuddering breath to steel her nerves, she tried to paste on a smile. "Sure Clay." Her sudden change of response seemed to take him off guard as his grip on her arms loosened slightly.

"That's more like it." He bent his head down to kiss her. She closed her eyes trying to take her mind to a different place. The revulsion for him made her stomach churn. Whiskey, she needed whiskey.

"How 'bout a drink?" Katy asked breaking away from the kiss trying to look like she wasn't trying to run again and tried to smile. "I have a bottle of whiskey in the kitchen I keep for jus' such an occasion."

He paused for a second as if contemplating her offer, his grip slackened a little again as his cold gaze bore into her. She tried not to wince and let him see her fear. The hunting rifle still hung only a few feet behind her. Could she move fast enough?

Before she could take a step he drew her in close again. "Nah. I don't feel like mixin' my drinkin' and women today. Besides I'm not in the mood for waitin'."

Katy mentally cursed her luck. He began fumbling with her buttons. It was the same shirt he'd ripped the buttons off last time. She'd sewn the buttons back stronger this time, but as his fingers didn't seem to work as fast as he wanted them he grasped each side and yanked hard. This time she heard ripping fabric. The fear in her chest turned to chills as he exposed her. A yelp escaped her lips.

He glared at her for a second and mumbled something before going back to ravaging her body. She closed her eyes and a willed herself to a different place. Tears she didn't know she had slid down her cheeks.

It'd been so long since he'd last made an appearance that she'd thought he'd leave her alone, but now she saw there would be no end to it. If he returned once he'd return again. Jess wouldn't stop him. He'd most likely blame her or worse. He might turn her over to him just to watch her misery.

Maybe she should tell him, then they might kill each other. That would take care of both her problems. If only one of them died that would still leave at least one of them to torment her and his revenge for telling or for falling prey would be even worse than now. She had to find an escape. There was no other way. She couldn't keep on like this.

The whiskey bottle was in her hands by the time the last clop of Clay's horse was heard leaving. The tears had dried on her face leaving salty streaks. Clay had used her as he willed then walked away just as casually as if he'd just brushed down his horse.

Drinking the first deep sip from the bottle helped dull her fears. She'd scurried away as soon as he'd freed her and put on the other pair of clothes she had. As she pressed her lips to the bottle and took another gulp of the fiery liquid, a rage began to burn in her. Who were these men that controlled her life by fear? She never got a chance to wear her fine dresses she'd bought anymore. They hung on a hook collecting dust. She dressed like a man all the time now. If she had to dress like a man then she would act like one too. The rage boiling her blood slowed as another shot of fire poured down her throat.

As the shades of darkness began to take over the landscape, Katy stumbled into the cabin after taking a lot longer than usual to do her daily chores. She could barely walk. She didn't hear the approach of a horse a few minutes after she'd gone inside, she was still trying to light the lamp that hung dark in the kitchen.

"Katy? Are you here?" That voice. Katy paused with the match stick in her fingers. The lamp lit finally as she stood there trying to figure out if the voice she heard was one that should frighten her or not. Her muddled head wouldn't let her think. The fire on the thin stick sped up and bit her fingers. A muttered curse escaped as she dropped it on the floor and stomped it out. At least she had a light now.

The door opened and she turned to see who it was. Pete came around the corner into the light.

"Katy! What happened?" He rushed up to her pulling her into him as she stood staring at him.

"You wanna toke meek moo?" Kind blue eyes searched her in confusion.

"What? You're mumblin' and you reek of whiskey."

Licking her lips, fighting to get the cotton out of her mouth, she tried to speak clearly. "You. Want. To. Take. Me. Too?" His expression clouded. "Everybody else does why not you? I not good enough for you?"

"Katy, tell me what happened. You're drunk and I'm don't know what you're talkin' about." Pete put his hands on her arms and bent slightly to look directly at her.

"Clay came back."

Thunderclouds formed across Pete's face. "I'll kill 'im. I swear I'll kill 'im"

A dopey smile put itself on her face. "You can't 'cause then Jess would find out what both of you have been doin' and he'd kill you and me both, but maybe that's better than livin' like this." She reached for the bottle she'd left on the table, but it was too far away with Pete blocking her.

A heavy sigh reached her ears. At first she wasn't sure if it came from her or from him. The pained looked on Pete's face as he stared up at the ceiling, as if searching for answers, made her think it'd come from him. She drooped against him as the effects of the alcohol became harder and harder to bear. She felt herself being lifted up, her head lulled against a strong shoulder, before being placed on a soft surface. Then everything went black.

CHAPTER 21

Empty blue eyes turned to Rex. A twitch at the corner of her mouth looked like she was trying to smile, but her face was still hollow and empty.

"I don't have to stay here anymore. There's no one to hunt me down. I can go wherever and do whatever I please." Her gaze shifted to Jess's lifeless form.

Thinking to tell her she'd still have to face trial, he pondered what she'd told him, yet after everything that'd transpired, he didn't think she'd mind jail too much. It would make taking her back to Fort Smith easier since she was willing to go. However, there was only a shell left of what he remembered of his sister. The tragedy that sat before him was something he'd never fully comprehended in his short career as a deputy marshal. Faced with it so close to home his understanding became all too real.

This was his sister. The little girl he swore to protect years ago when their house had burned down during the war by bushwhackers, after which they'd moved to Fort Smith. He'd failed. She sat there broken and unfeeling.

His mind flashed back to a girl with sunny smiles and tinkling, sweet laughter that filled the air with sunshine. She was ten and he was a gangly sixteen. They'd been picking blackberries near the creek and he'd slipped and fallen into the prickly bush trying to get a particularly fat berry that eluded him. It felt like only days ago, yet it'd been a lifetime for them both.

Nothing of that time remained. They were both changed. Both of them scarred from life. He had no words of comfort for her. What was there to say? Rex shook his head, his blond hair shifting ever so slightly with the movement, staring into the darkness beyond the fire. That darkness had swallowed them whole. It had crept into their heads, then their hearts. Light was only a word, like the stars in the sky, only specks to be looked at from afar. Too much evil had taken over this world. Too many good people had been hurt and changed forever.

The afternoon sun burned bright with a reminder that summer was near and promised little relief from the heat. Katy felt the effects of her drinking binge the night before. Her head was fuzzy and a faint throb at her temples made movement painful. She'd been roused out of her sleep when Pete had left again in the grey light of dawn. Barely able to recall his coming, she more than felt the ache of his leaving. When he was with her she felt protected and when he left she didn't just feel vulnerable, she knew it. Yesterday had more than proved that. She would carry the hunting rifle, or any kind of weapon she could keep on her person, with her wherever she went now. She couldn't relive another day like that. The small caliber pistol Jess usually had her carry on their *business ventures* was a spare he kept in his saddle bags whenever he went out on his own.

The pounding in her head grew in intensity, or was that a horse coming? Focusing her energy at placing the noise she soon saw Jess coming toward her. His face was usually impassive, but this time he looked more agitated. He should be elated after coming back from his debauchery with Pale Moon. What had happened? Not that she cared about either, but depending on what had transpired could take its aftermath directly out on her.

"Who's been here?" Jess growled by way of greeting as he stopped his horse directly in front of her.

Her muddled head kept the fear out of her eyes, or at least she hoped it would. Looking up with a blank face she hoped she wouldn't have to explain about Pete, or Clay for that matter.

When she didn't answer right away and continued to give him a blank stare, he dismounted and walked up to her, a deep scowl wrinkling what she'd once thought were handsome features, but now only conjured feeling of ill contempt.

"I saw two different sets of horse tracks when I came in. Who you been entertainin'? You lettin' other men steal my place in my own bed?"

"What? No." Fear crept up her spine as she watched his temper rise as the color of his face darkened. "Clay and Pete both came by lookin' for you. I told them you weren't here and they left right away."

The hand that knocked her into the dust told her he didn't believe her. Pain ripped through her head until she thought it would split open onto the ground.

"I swear nothin' happened." The break in her voice seemed to please him. "Ask them. They'll tell you the truth." She pleaded hoping to save herself from another onslaught of his anger.

"I will ask them, and if either of 'em tells me any different, then I guess I'll have to remind 'im and you who you belong to." He patted the butt of his gun that hung close to his waist. She only hoped they'd give him a similar version of the story as she had.

With a splitting headache, a fat lip, and clothes full of dust, Katy managed to stand and walk into the house to perform her wifely tasks hoping to melt, forgotten, into the shadows.

Leaning against a tree with the contents of her stomach at her feet, Katy waited for the waves of nausea to subside taking as small of breaths as possible, afraid of angering her already churning stomach. Her hair hung limp and stray strands plastered themselves against her face. This was the fourth day in a row she'd found herself in such a vulnerable position. At first she thought she'd fallen ill, but as the day wore on she began to feel fine. The next morning it was the same thing. Trying to keep Jess from finding out, she would barely make it out of the house in the morning before the sickness accosted her again.

Staring at the ground around her feet she felt the cold fingers of truth grip her. This was her worst nightmare staring her in the face. They were due to ride out next week on another stage hold-up. Somebody was bound to figure out what was wrong and then there'd be hell to pay. How could she hide it from five men when she could barely escape one each morning? Maybe she could fake an illness and Jess would let her stay home? No, he might send Pale Moon to care for her, or most likely spy on her, if she were to stay back. That was the last person she wanted checking on her, especially since she would probably see the signs and go running to Jess telling him the truth. No, that was out of the question. She'd rather brave five men than that one woman.

With a final deep breath to steady herself, Katy turned back to her chores before she was discovered. The nausea subsided just long enough to keep her from doubling over again. Maybe she'd be better by next week and her problem would solve itself. Maybe.

Nothing had changed in the passing week. Katy cursed under her breath as she saw Rick riding in from her hiding place that had become her "sick tree". Her time was up this morning. She took a great gulp of fresh air and a small sip of water from a cup she'd begun bringing with her hoping to steady herself before facing the first of the gang. Wiping the sweat plastered hair from her face she hoped she didn't look as bad as she felt or her secret would be transparent.

Darting back inside, she started the coffee she knew all the men would be looking for as they trickled in. Her stomach began to gurgle and roll, she mentally scolded it to calm down and get quiet.

Jess walked into the kitchen fastening his belt as he turned to Rick who waited at the kitchen table.

"Mornin' Rick. How's our prospects lookin' this time?"

"From what I've heard we may have a small payroll comin' if we can get there in time."

"Good." Jess slapped Rick on the back heartily before pulling up a chair himself. "What's takin' that coffee so long woman? Ain't you been up long enough to have that done yet?"

At the sharp accusation Katy's stomach gave a lurch threatening to spill her secret all over the kitchen. Struggling to keep control of her insides, she ignored the men and let them talk and plan.

Instead she took one slow breath at a time focusing on the coffee and breathing to keep her upright.

Before the coffee was finished the sound of another horse reached to the occupants inside the house.

"Pull up a seat." Jess invited as Morgan's shadow blocked the doorway, swirling his hat in his hands. "We're jus' waitin' on coffee that seems slower than molasses today."

Morgan shot a quick glance through the kitchen doorway at Katy, before he turned his attention back to Jess.

"Whitey.. I .. uh.. I didn't take Ginny to Pale Moon this time. She's stayin' at our place alone."

Silence filled the room like billowing smoke. Katy's hand froze above the coffee pot she was about to take off the small iron stove, not daring to make a sound as she listened to how Jess would respond.

She couldn't blame Ginny for not wanting to go stay with Pale Moon. Her heart tightened at the thought of the little blonde haired girl staying all alone while they were gone. What if something happened to Morgan while they were gone? What if he was arrested and jailed? What if he was killed? What would happen to the girl?

"Why didn't she go?" The question sounded harmless enough, but Katy knew if she turned around she'd see Jess's eyes boring into Morgan like spikes.

"She didn't want to go." Morgan glanced at the wood floor before looking back up again, his hat spinning faster in his hands. "She threw such a fit when I told her it was time to go that I couldn't do anythin' with her."

Another pause filled the room. Katy risked looking over her shoulder at Morgan, who looked nervous and miserable. He took another deep breath before pressing on. "And she's... well she's been havin' nightmares again since I started sendin' her to Pale Moon while I'm gone. I didn't have the heart to make her go again. I don't have a problem with Pale Moon, but Ginny's nightmares after her parents' deaths...." His voice trailed off as he failed to find a way to describe his problem.

Katy made a vow to herself then that she would start taking the time out of her nightmarish life to go visit Ginny. Ginny needed an older white woman to be close to her, and Katy needed a diversion from her own nightmares that happened waking or sleeping.

From where she stood Katy couldn't see Jess's reaction on his face, but the rigged set of his back looked like a cat ready to pounce.

"I'm sure she'll be fine. We'll ride past Pale Moon's on our way out and let her know Ginny won't be comin'." Jess replied. Morgan's hat suddenly stilled. All the anxiety in the room seemed to fade in a second. Except for Katy's. Her skinned crawled. A new wave of nausea washed over her. She'd get a chance first hand to see Pale Moon.

The men settled in while Katy poured their coffee. Pete drifted in by the end of the first cup. Clay finally showed at the end of the second cup of coffee, looking more rumpled than usual. Katy didn't care. She was trying hard not to look at Pete and avoiding all of them, in general. The nausea had passed and she was just beginning to feel human again when they all walked out to saddle up. Her feet felt heavy thinking about coming face to face with Pale Moon.

A short while later, the six of them rode into a small clearing with a small log cabin in the center. It looked ordinary enough. Katy pulled her hat down lower over her eyes. Her stomach was in knots again, threatening her delicate balance with every step of the horse. She let her horse drift further to the back of the group. Jess appeared to have forgotten she existed as he nudged his horse into a slow trot.

The door to the small cabin opened. Katy sucked in a breath as she stared at the dark haired beauty that walked out. The dark haired woman had to be at least three inches taller than her. A lithe body, fully feminine, was plain to see despite the mix of traditional and westernized clothing she wore. The dark eyes and flawless skin would be enough to make any man turn his head no matter what color he was. Katy squeezed her eyes shut trying to stop her panic. No wonder Jess kept going back to her.

Warm breath tickled her elbow. She opened her eyes. A horse's nose nudged her. Looking back, Pete sat behind her on his horse. A flash of pity showed in his eyes for a fleeting second before he pulled his horse back and walked past her, his face once again a mask.

Straightening her back, Katy reminded herself that she no longer cared what Jess did or who he saw. She had someone who cared for her, even if it was impossible to be together. Her shoulders sagged as the next thought that crossed her mind was that no one would care for her, once they all knew she was pregnant.

Jess's back was toward her when she halted her mare just out of ear shot. Pale Moon put a slender hand on his knee in a familiar gesture as they spoke. No sign of emotion crossed her face as he spoke to her. Katy barely caught the fleeting glance that Pale Moon sent her way just before she turned back toward the small cabin.

Minutes later, a trail of dust was following the band of renegades as they rode off. Katy wondered at the fact that she had no feelings at that point. She should be mad, or at the very least she should be disgusted with Jess, but there was nothing. Unconsciously, she followed along, lost in her own thoughts. The job ahead did not hold the fear for her life that was normally there; in fact she began to wonder if a stray bullet was not the way to end all her problems.

CHAPTER 22

Rex looked over to his broken sister. He couldn't imagine the pain she'd felt, or even still was feeling. He'd never had to face the demons in his own soul; there'd always been others to take down instead. His own struggles seemed so small in comparison. The fact that she'd not committed suicide and was seated beside him attested to her inner strength that he was convinced she was unaware that she possessed. Ma would say it was by the grace of God that they'd finally crossed paths and he was now in a position to save her, again.

A wisp of hair escaped her hat. Gently he took her hat from her head. The still air left her hair as limp as she was. He tucked the loose strand behind her ear away from her face. Her eyes were dry. He realized then he could deal with her tears better than this, this empty shell left of his sister.

When they were young, Ma had let them go down to the creek to swim one summer. He was a strong swimmer and Katy still clung closely to the bank afraid to go out on her own. It was after a long rain, the waters were up more than usual. Rex was out near the middle when a shriek pierced the air. He'd turned around just in time to see Katy's head bob under the water. With strength and speed he didn't know he possessed, he'd swam against the current to her rescue. Pulling her shaking, sputtering, and crying from the swift moving water, he'd found his footing, half dragging her from the creek.

She'd cried for what felt like hours that day realizing how close she'd come to drowning. It'd shaken him as well. The tears afterward insignificant as he had shed a few of his own there in the tall grass beside the creek, her head cradled on his shoulder. He could handle that. He could handle the tears, the anger, the sadness. This, this was entirely different. He wanted blood, but he'd already been cheated of that. He wanted to turn the clock back and still have the same little sister he remembered.

"What kept you goin'?" Rex asked quietly.

"I'm not sure. At that point I was almost completely unfeeling. I'd been betrayed, lied to, misguided, naïve, and yet I knew it couldn't end there. There's gotta be somethin' else for me besides this. There's got to be another way. By the time we got to our camp that night I knew the only way to change things were to do it myself. Death was not an option. I couldn't cheat and go the easy way out. If someone was goin' to die it wasn't goin' to be me."

Tying her mount to a tree near camp, Katy inadvertently looked around for a place to hide in the morning when she knew the waves of nausea would hit. The long, dark fingers that were the shadows of evening hid any good places to hide come morning. With resignation, Katy lifted her bedroll off her horse and turned back to camp. Morning would probably bring her undoing. If she was lucky Jess would just kill her there. At worst he'd leave her to her own devices here in the middle of Indian Territory, lost, alone, and hopeless. She might be able to track her way to a road, but where would she go? She had nowhere to call home. She couldn't face Ma. Why would she take her back anyway? She was a tainted woman.

Tonight would be the last night they would use a fire until they got back from their mission. Katy took the meager rations of beans they'd brought and attempted to turn it into something edible without gagging on the smell.

Wondering if the slurping from the men would bring the law down on their heads before morning, Katy sat back quietly in the shadows on a fallen log trying to force the beans into her stomach without them returning. Jess was deep in conversation with Rick in front of her close to the fire, each of their plates emptying faster than they were talking. An occasional word would drift back to her like "strong box", "guard", "problems". It didn't instill a sense of optimism, but she didn't care. In fact, she was tempted to hope their robbery failed. However, the way things were shaping up, it would be Pete or Morgan that was shot, not Clay or Jess. Rick, well she didn't care either way what happened to him.

Taking another deep breath she willed the waves of nausea away after swallowing another bite of beans. She stared at her plate. Feeling Pete's eyes on her wasn't helping. She didn't dare look up, didn't dare look into his eyes, afraid the truth would be written across her face. He couldn't do anything to help. It wasn't his fault she was in this position. He was just as helpless of a pawn as she.

Pleading a headache, Katy turned in early. The low cadence of the men's voices carried to the edge of her consciousness as she drifted into a troubled sleep.

Soft grey tendrils of dawn played across the sky when she opened her eyes. Listening for evidence of any of the others moving around, she heard nothing, not even the birds were awake. Sitting up slowly, she checked bedrolls. They were all full. Counting to ten waiting for the onslaught of nausea to hit, with her feet untangling themselves from the bedroll, she bolted into the woods as silently and as far away as she could get before finding the biggest tree to empty the contents of her stomach behind.

After her stomach was empty, she made her way back to camp with sluggish steps. A touch to her elbow made her jump, a scream caught in her throat. Whirling around she came face to face with Pete.

"What happened? Why are you so far out in the woods today?" His soft voice calming her heart from the scare he'd given her.

"Jus' needed some privacy this mornin'." The men usually left her alone so she didn't have to wonder so far from camp for her necessary needs.

Piercing blue eyes washed over her, disbelief clearly visible on his face. Looking at the ground, unable to meet his gaze, she hoped the pallor of her face was not clear in the early morning shadows.

"Be careful." He whispered, his gaze pointedly on the missing gun belt that was still in her saddle bag.

Making it back to camp before any of the others woke up, Katy steeled herself for another day, the hardest part was over.

The early signs of evening were crowding the woods with shadows and taking some of the warmth out of the clear sky. A chill swept up Katy's spine as the heavy sounds of wheels approached. Being stationed farthest from the road also meant being farthest from the action, which, when considered, wasn't a bad thing except meaning she couldn't readily see what was happening either.

Faint sounds and movement were all she could see from her vantage point. She waited for the telltale gunshot that would take a life.

A horse stomped its foot behind her. The team she held the reigns to were a restless lot. Giving a sharp jerk to the reigns she hoped they'd quiet down. The leader of the pack, Rick's horse, gave a sharp snort in her direction. She glared back at it, the contest of wills between human and animal intense as the seconds ticked by.

A discernible thud echoed through the shallow woods, making her turn her head first. It was probably the stage's strong box she thought, without a gunshot it couldn't be a body falling. Aside from a few muffled shouts from Jess, the job seemed to be running smoothly. She wasn't sure how that made her really feel.

The horses had quieted as they seemed to be listening too. A flicker of an ear here and there made Katy think they could hear and understand what was going on better than she.

The men with bandanna covered faces and hats pulled low over their eyes were moving around the stage coach as quick as they could. Morgan had back hold duty, checking bags of luggage. Clay was perched on top of the stage keeping an eye on the driver and passengers from behind. Rick was taking up collections from the passengers with Jess standing to the side, rifle trained on the driver. Pete emptied the strong box that seemed smaller than the last.

Katy frowned. If this strike wasn't good enough the next would come sooner or Jess might change again back to bank robbery, or even try handling both. It was not a thought she relished. She couldn't go on much longer without the obvious signs of her conditions being self evident and when she no longer held a use for Jess, would he keep her around or would he discard her by the way side.

Clay started to climb down from his perch on the stage coach. That was her cue. She jabbed her heel into her mount and led the rest of the horses behind her to collect the men. The familiar rush she got when they fled the scene was beginning to surge through her blood. Would they all make it safely away without a bullet in the back like Pete after the last bank job? She shook her head. Those kinds of thoughts made reality happen in the worst kinds of ways.

Breaking through the woods at a lope, the men scrambled to load their loot and hoist their bodies onto their horses. Jess walked backward as his men started off. The last one mounted. Jess pointed his rifle in the general direction over the stage and pulled the trigger. As the passengers ducked down, Jess grabbed reign and sunk spur. Katy hunkered low near the mane of her horse, the rough hair flying in her face, as she followed on the heels of Jess's horse.

CHAPTER 23

"What happened to the baby Katy?" Rex didn't want to ask the question, afraid of what the answer would be. He'd known women who'd lost babies, especially when they lived rough lives. He'd seen the toll it'd taken on their bodies, and their minds, but he had to ask. He had to know it was a simple natural course of things, that Jess hadn't beaten her until she lost it. At least he'd assumed she'd lost it. The timing, as he knew it, said it'd come too early and, without proper care, easily perished. There were no proper doctors that he knew of in the vicinity. His heart squeezed at the thoughts of his sister with no one to care for her in one of greatest times of need.

Her body went rigged at his question. Risking a glance at her, Rex saw her gulping air trying to tamp down a fresh set of tears. From the look on her face, he knew it was the wrong question to ask. Her mask of anger dropped to one of total anguish. Closing his eyes and shaking his head, he knew he was going to like this part of her story even less. Wrapping his arms around her, he pulled her close.

The temptation to reach for the ever present whiskey bottle was strong tonight, but something her mother had said years ago, about pregnant women who drank having poor babies, kept her from reaching for it. She had enough troubles as it was, she couldn't handle a hard birth or a baby in poor health, but that didn't help the dark shadows and nightmares go away.

Exhaustion tugged at her, the dark circles under her eyes betraying her efforts to be brave. She'd awoken at every little sound the night made after Jess had left for his rendezvous with Pale Moon. Tonight was her second night alone. At least the days were slowly getting longer, so the nights didn't keep their terrifying grip on her quite as long.

A knock at the door startled Katy from her deep, brooding thoughts. The mud from the rains that had delayed Jess's departure yesterday muffled the hoof beats of her visitor. She hated surprises. This time she would be ready.

Grabbing the hunting rifle from above the fire place, she walked within range of the door and aimed.

"Come in." Katy ordered in her strongest voice. If it was Clay she would have no qualms about

223

shooting him tonight. At least one of her nightmares would be over.

The slight creak of the door echoed ominously through the small cabin as it swung open on its hinges. Cocking the hammer as a dark shape materialized in the door frame, Katy steadied her aim.

"Don't shoot. It's me." The familiar welcoming voice was like a cool breeze on a hot day.

Katy disengaged the gun as it nearly fell to the floor with her relief. Her shoulders sagged, the rest of her body threatened to follow. Strong arms caught her and helped her back to her chair.

"Don't scare me like that. Next time call out or something." Katy half scolded as Pete walked back to the rifle and put it in its place about the fireplace.

"Sorry. I wasn't thinkin'. You usually hear me." He apologized, looking somewhat sheepish.

She waved a hand at him dismissively. "I'm a little edgy. I've left the whiskey alone so there's nothin' to calm my nerves, and well, frankly I'm scared to death."

"More so than usual?" His blue eyes, that appeared soft moments before in the warm firelight, came sharp and alert.

A heavy sigh escaped before she could catch it. He was too perceptive. She couldn't tell him her terrible secret though, but what if he found out later without her telling him? What would he say then? He would hate her. What would he do if she told him now? Could things get any worse? No, that was not a good thought to explore.

"Maybe, a little." She conceded. The internal war with her secret and the only man who had seemed to care for her seemed to be in a stale mate.

Squatting on his knees beside her chair, he placed a rough, tanned hand on hers as he looked directly into her eyes. She couldn't look away, his gentleness with her made her resolve buckle.

"I have a terrible secret." The words caught in her throat and she looked away.

"Well, I'm assumin' it's not that you killed Jess. I saw his horse where it usually is." He was trying to lighten the mood and yet not say too much about the whole situation.

The corner of her mouth quirked at his suggestion of killing Jess. If she were totally honest with herself she knew the thought had crossed her mind once in one of the dark, whiskey laden nights she'd spent alone.

"No. I.." Taking a deep breath and swallowing all her fears, she plunged ahead. "I'm with child."

The silence of the cabin made her risk a glance at Pete. His face was unreadable.

"I figured it out a little over a month ago. I haven't told Jess. I've been afraid. I don't know how he'll react. What should I do?" She rushed on, her voice threatening to crack.

Silence hung in the air as he glanced at the floor, seeming to search for an answer. Finally, he looked back up at her.

"You have to stay. You have to tell him. Maybe this is what he needs to get himself together. Has he beaten you since you found out?" She shook her head. She'd made sure to stay clear of him. "You know you can't hide it much longer. Have you been sick or anything?"

"I've been sick in the mornings. That's how I figured it out, otherwise I probably wouldn't have known for a long time. Ma really never had much chance to tell me 'bout these things. I was the youngest and we had no younger family members to care for. I barely know anything and I'm scared. Who will care for me way out here? How can I do it alone?"

"There's women who Whitey can ask to care for you. He surely knows someone. How've you managed to hide…" he paused as a light seem to flicker in his head. "That's what you were doin' so far in the woods when we did that last job isn't it?"

She nodded.

"I don't know what to tell you, except the longer you keep it a secret from Whitey the madder he'll be when he finds out. You should know he hates havin' anythin' kept from him."

Katy felt miserable. She slumped further into the hard wooden chair. He hadn't offered to run away with her like he'd suggested when he first found out how ruthless Jess was to her. In fact, he was telling her to stay with her nightmare.

After a minute he moved to a chair near her, the silence stretched long. The shadows no longer haunted her. Instead of the comforting presence she normally felt being near Pete, she was angry. Who was he to pretend he cared for her and yet tell her to stay with the man who beat her? Who was he to tell her anything?

"You need to leave now." The words spoken so quietly in the over charged silence of the room seemed to echo like thunder when Pete turned his gaze on her.

For the first time that night, she saw the pain in his eyes. The façade had dropped and she realized he was in as much turmoil as she. It was too late now. She'd made up her mind. If he wouldn't rescue her now, he never would. Why hope in something that so obviously was only a dream? She would face what she had to on her own. She didn't need any false sympathy or pretty words. She was the only one who was to blame for her predicament and she was the only one who could do anything about it.

"Katy. I.."

"Out. Now." Cutting off his words, she pointed toward the door. She was done, done with it all.

Stuffing his hat down hard on his head, he stalked to the door, turned, his mouth working like words were trying to come out. For a fleeting second she dared to hope he was going to invite her to go with him, instead he turned without a word and walked into the dark night.

"What's goin' on? You ain't been drinkin' yer whiskey like you were?" Jess stood dangling her nearly full jug of whiskey between his fingers in front of him.

Katy turned away from the stove, her eyes focused on the brown jug.

"I jus' haven't really been feelin' it much lately." Without looking him in the eye, she tried to sound convincing.

In one long stride he crossed the room to her, grasping a handful of her loose hair he yanked back, making her look up at his face.

"Yer lyin'." She felt like a cornered rabbit. It'd been over two months since she'd found out about her predicament and knew her time for hiding was running out. Pete's words echoed in her ears as she looked up into the dark menacing eyes that she'd once thought she'd fallen in love with.

"No. Jess really. I.. I have a reason." She stuttered, his grip on her hair tightening. She wasn't ready to deal with it. Maybe he would treat her more kindly if she told him. With that small fragment of hope she went on. "I'm with child."

Registering shock for only a split second, his face quickly turned dark with rage.

"You dirty, filthy whore! Who's is it? Do you even know?" The words were spoken in a low voice, but with enough venom to kill a viper.

"Y-yours. Who else's would it be?" Katy was stunned. How could he think she was seeing other men and when he was constantly visiting Pale Moon, who was he to call her names?

"Liar!" He roared flinging her one handed to the ground. A few hairs had wrapped around his fingers and were yanked out as she fell.

A startled cry erupted from her mouth that she'd meant to keep in.

"Get up." Switching the whiskey bottle to his other hand, he waited for her to obey.

Fear held her in its grips. She wondered briefly if he was going to kill her right there in the kitchen in the middle of cooking dinner. With shaky legs, she managed to stand facing him.

Running his free hand along her abdomen, chills ran up her spine with foreboding. She watched, feeling like she was looking down at someone else, as his fist reared back before slamming into her stomach. Air whooshed from her lungs at the impact. For a second, she was afraid she was going to vomit on him as the pain coursed through her. Doubling over, she gulped for air.

"That should take care of any bastard living inside of you." His cold words wrapped their tentacles' around her. "And hurry up with the food. I'm hungry." Taking a slug out of her whiskey bottle, he brushed past her and walked into the living room like nothing had happened.

Tears slid unwillingly down her cheeks. Her entire body hurt even though her breathing had returned to almost normal. A salty tear splashed into her pan and sizzled with the heat. If Jess's method for making her miscarry worked, she'd leave the next time he visited Pale Moon. She'd have nothing holding her back. The worst that could happen would be she died and right now that was a most welcoming thought. She couldn't take the pain anymore. If she couldn't escape it she'd die trying.

The rest of the evening light cramps racked her body. Jess had drunk himself into a stupor and sat slouched over in his chair. She wondered if she was dying when the blood had begun a short while earlier. As she lay down in the bed to sleep, she wondered if she would wake in the morning or would die quietly in her sleep. She'd heard tales of women who'd bled to death in child birth. This could be the last thought she had before she died, she marveled.

It felt strange knowing this could be her last day on earth. She thought about Ma and Rex, wondering if they'd ever find out what happened to her. She remembered the black clad preacher telling them about hell from the pulpit. Would the faith she thought she had so long ago open the gates of heaven for her now? She'd lived her hell on earth. Surely anything was worse than this.

Katy closed her eyes, at peace.

CHAPTER 24

The landscape turned red as anger swept through Rex like a roaring fire. The fact she was alive and talking to him did nothing to damper his rage. He brushed away a tear of anger that pooled in the corner of his eye.

"I lived." Those two simple words spoken without emotion fell like a rock between them.

She had lived. How, he didn't know. For a fleeting second, he wondered if she wouldn't have been happier if she'd had died. Slamming his eyes shut against the idea, he shook his head violently wondering what had possessed him to even think that. He needed her alive. Ma needed her alive. Even though her condition was so terribly deteriorated, she was alive. If he'd have found out she'd died it would've destroyed Ma and him both.

Emotionally charged words sputtered from his mouth, barely making it past the lump of sadness forming in his throat. "I'm so glad you did too." Without restraint he hugged her close, swallowing back tears that he furiously blinked away. "Somebody has to be around to keep me in line." He attempted to jest with her when she didn't respond.

Red rimmed eyes, so guileless and empty focused on him. Her lower lip began to quiver. He wanted her to cry. He needed to know she was still capable of emotion that she wasn't completely broken.

Someone was breathing heavily near her face making her hair move. The sharp smell of stale liquor made her stomach roil reminding her of the nightmare that was her life. Blinking her eyes open she wondered why she hadn't died. She'd been ready.

Jess sat leaning heavily over the bed in her face. Her night dress was pulled up revealing her legs. With a huge amount of effort she tried to push it into place. Did she still carry the child? She didn't know how she would know either way.

"Good yer awake. I have a new plan." Malevolence glowed from his eyes.

Another roll of her stomach had her attempting to jump from bed to run for her "sick tree". Jess caught her arm in a vice like grip.

"Where you goin'?" His words were still slightly slurred.

The little bit of food she'd managed to eat last night started creeping up her throat. Slapping a hand across her mouth in a useless gesture to keep it down, she couldn't speak for fear of erupting.

"Get dressed. We have someplace to go."

Wide eyes greeted him, as she frantically looked for a place to empty out at, that wasn't on him. She didn't want to think about the beating she would take if that should happen. Spotting the wash basin in the corner of the room, she pointed, hoping he'd let her go before the smell of him made her lose control.

He let her arm go and she fled across the room barely reaching the small basin in time.

When she was finally empty, her stomach hurt more than ever. She was drained physically and emotionally. Jess watched her with his viper like eyes as she tried to straighten herself and get her bearing back.

"We're leavin' in five minutes. Be ready." He stood and walked out of the room. Katy noticed the brown jug of whiskey still dangled from his fingertips.

With each plod of her mare's hoof, pain racked her body. She couldn't even focus long enough to think about where they might be going. She could barely stay in the saddle.

The pain had numbed her senses to the point she no longer felt anything. The horses carried them into a small clearing. It took a moment for it to register where they were.

It was Pale Moon's cabin. What on earth had he brought her here for? Her muddled mind couldn't come up with any possibilities.

Jess's usual fluid movements seemed wobbly and jerky as he dismounted his horse and approached the door of the cabin. His hand was poised to knock when it opened. Katy still sat back, rooted in place.

Words were exchanged in low voices before Jess turned to look for her. His scowl deepened as he saw how far back she sat.

"Come here." He ordered as Pale Moon ducked into the cabin. They were going to kill her here. It would be much less obvious here than at their cabin she realized. This morning she wasn't sure how she felt about dying. Last night it'd seemed easy and painless, but sitting here staring at the cabin she knew pain awaited her in force.

After a hesitant moment trying to make her mind obey the command, she nudged her mare ahead bringing her closer to certain death. Her limbs felt weighted, the pain that had continually wracked her body had also numbed her brain. Her body protested every movement she made as she slowly slid off her mount. Instead of a reassuring hand to catch her as she stood on shaky legs, Jess roughly took hold of her arm, leading her into the small cabin.

The dark clouds overhead that threatened rain seemed much less ominous than this one room cabin. Through the dull light that filtered in the windows, Katy noted the single bed in the corner, draped in a colorfully patterned Indian style blanket. Her stomach recoiled in disgust as the thought of the other two occupants use of it. A small wooden table with two chairs sat near the opposite side of the room where a few pots, pans, and ladles were hung. Herbs and other possibly nourishing substances hung from the ceiling. In her daze, Katy looked around and realized all the cooking was done over the fireplace.

For a brief moment, the image of Ma cooking at a fireplace stirred her memory. When they'd moved in with her Aunt Stella during the War Between the States, she'd had a real stove that Ma learned to cook on. Funny she should remember that now. She'd only been six at the time, and only recently had to do much cooking of her own. In her past life, as she thought of it, she'd always been needed somewhere besides the kitchen as Ma held firm control of the family's stomach.

Turning her gaze from the flickering fireplace, she came to the understanding that it was one of the few things she didn't envy of Pale Moon. The rest of the room held very little. What a lonely life Katy thought. The irony of that thought soon caught up to her. Maybe the thoughts of Ma and Aunt Stella had caused her to briefly feel cherished. They loved her and cared for her, she knew, well, at least they had until they found out what she'd become. They wouldn't take her back now, even if she didn't die today.

With that realization, her wondering mind came back to reality, watching as Pale Moon was busying herself with a small bowl at the table. She had some vials and plants taken from their hanging place, arrayed on the flat surface. Katy still stood barely inside the doorway. Jess had propped himself up against the frame behind her as though he was guarding her exit.

Noticing her glance back to him, a ruthless smile that turned his eyes to stone, spread across his face.

"Pull up a chair. I don't know how long this'll take." He motioned to the two chairs sitting near where Pale Moon worked in silence as though he was inviting a guest in for polite conversation.

Was she watching Pale Moon create something that would kill her? She bit down the panic that threatened to overwhelm her, but as much as she tried to think of another reason why Jess would bring her here, nothing came to mind. The quiet that settled around the room while Pale Moon worked felt evil and foreboding. The shadows of the room emanated darkness of a different kind, sinister in its feel.

Many of the herbs that lay strewn across the table where unfamiliar to Katy. She wished she'd watched Aunt Stella more as a child when she helped treat wounded soldiers during the war. Aunt Stella had a gift for medicine, as Ma had put it. She knew how to cure practically anything. "Here dearie drink this" or "let me rub this on you". Katy couldn't remember a time Aunt Stella's treatments didn't work, well except for Pa although the doctor said nothing could cure his heart. For a moment, she almost let herself grieve for Pa as the ache of his passing washed over her, but she wouldn't let herself give in. This was not the time to allow weakness.

As Katy sat there thinking of her aunt, she could hear her voice in her head. She closed her eyes and let herself remember. Her memories were tinged with regret. She remembered feeling cared for by both of the strong women in her life, Ma and Aunt Stella. Both had lost husbands, yet they found the strength to carry on. If only she herself could find the strength to escape her current predicament. If only she could live past today, she might be able to find a way. The memories filled her mind as one door opened to another. She was in no hurry to open her eyes because it might be the last time she'd get to remember anything.

A stirring beside her brought Katy crashing out of her memories. It could've been minutes, it could have been hours, she had no way of knowing. Her eyes had adjusted to the light of the room, even with Jess's shadow cast over her from his imposing form as he stood beside her chair.

Pale Moon held a small bowl in her slender brown hands as she walked around the table toward them. In one last panicked moment Katy hoped to find an escape. It was no use. Even if she could somehow manage to bolt out the door or get through a window, she didn't know her way in this country. She could guess, but she knew Jess would catch up with her before she got out of the yard. Maybe if she could spill the potion there would be a shortage of herbs to mix another batch, buying her time to figure out a better escape plan.

"Drink this. It won't hurt you." Pale Moon stopped just out of arms reach from Katy, her voice calm and smooth. A look somewhere akin to pity crossed her face as she offered the bowl.

A cynical smirk creased Katy's mouth. Was she serious? They were about to kill her and she was expected to just go along with it. *It won't hurt.* It might not hurt but the result would be the same. She'd be dead.

Suddenly, a click sounded in the silence. Without looking, Katy knew Jess had sensed her twitch and pulled his gun on her. The cold steel was casually kissing her temple.

"We're takin' care of you're little problem once and for all. Drink what the lady is offerin' you and when it's all over you can come back to the cabin. It'll be like nothin' ever happened."

Katy was completely confused. What was he talking about? Little problem? Come back?

Taking advantage of the clear confusion playing across Katy's face, Pale Moon placed the small wooden bowl in Katy's lifeless hands.

"That's a good girl. Now drink it down." Jess motioned with the gun to the bowl then to her mouth. "I won't shoot you as long as you behave."

When Katy finally got up the nerve to look at him, the sneer in his voice matched the look at his face. The choice was simple. She didn't like pain and she'd seen enough bullet holes to know it was painful. If the herbal potion was painless to her then that's how she would die. No sense in making it difficult on herself.

With shaking hands, Katy lifted the small bowl to her lips. Trying not to focus too much on the smell, afraid of what it would taste like, she gulped it down like she had her first taste of whiskey, without a breath.

Handing the bowl back to Pale Moon without a word, afraid her voice would be as shaky as her hands, she wondered how long it would take to go into effect. Would she know she was dying or would she just gently drift off to sleep, never to awaken again?

Jess eased the hammer back into place and smiled, actually smiled almost pleasantly as if a burden had been lifted from him, as he placed the gun back into its holster. "Thatta girl. I knew you had it in you."

"I should prepare a place for her before it starts working." Pale Moon said gliding past them. Jess made himself comfortable in the nearby chair to Katy. His suddenly relax manner puzzled her. She would not be this calm if she was about to watch someone die, but then Pale Moon was going to prepare her burial place so it was unlikely he'd actually watch her die.

The eerie silence that had engulfed them before she drank the strange potion was back. There were no parting words she wished to say. Jess had turned out to be the worst thing to ever happen in her life. Once she'd thought he was the answer to her troubles, now in the dim light of the small cabin in Indian Territory she realized how terribly naïve she'd been.

Across the room Pale Moon was arranging her bed and seemed to be going to a lot of extra trouble with it. Katy opened her mouth to ask about her curious behavior, but just as she did so, a pang hit her stomach. It was then that she noticed the pain in her stomach had eased since they'd arrived.

Sadness washed over her as she understood she'd be unable to bring life to the small form within her, not that it'd have much to live for anyway, but all the same it was her duty to make the best of it.

A single tear slid down her cheek at the thoughts whirling around in her head. She didn't bother to brush it away. She felt like a stone, immobile, helpless. Another pain shot through her stomach, a little bit harder.

Turning from the bed, Pale Moon walked across the small space to Katy and stood before her carefully scrutinizing her when another pang hit. Pale Moon nodded.

"It's starting to work. Katy, come lay over here."

After a moment's hesitation, Katy stood on leaded legs and began walking across the room. She was only an arm's length from the bed when a stomach pain made her double over with pain.

"I-I thought you said this wouldn't hurt me." Katy gasped, speaking for the first time since she'd left her and Jess's cabin.

"I said it wouldn't hurt *you*, by that I meant you will live through it and be able bare children in the future."

Turning to sit on the bed, the realization of what was happening finally broke through her muddled thoughts. They'd forced her to drink something that would make her loose the baby. Blinking furiously to keep the tears from flowing, she sat there twice as miserable as before as another pang wracked her body.

"Please lay down. It will be easier." Pale Moon was being gentle with her, but her expression was blank, completely unreadable as to her present thoughts. Katy wondered again at the flicker of what she'd almost thought was pity that crossed the other woman's face earlier. She'd known all along what would happen.

Katy wanted to hate Pale Moon for what she'd done to her, but she remembered Jess and his use of the gun. Maybe Pale Moon was just as afraid of him as she was. As the pain continued to pound her body, she knew she was at Pale Moon's mercy no matter if she hated her or not.

The pain in her stomach continued to increase. It swelled, then for a split second it would ease before another shot of pain would grip her body. Katy bit her lip, refusing to scream as she wished to do, refusing to show weakness in front of this woman and the devil that put her here. It was bad enough she couldn't hold back the whimpering that escaped her lips, but she refused to cry out, she refused to cry, though she wished to do both.

Vengeance for her present state began to grow with each swelling of pain. When this was all over her pain filled mind swore, she'd find a way to escape. If she couldn't escape, she'd seek the vengeance she deserved.

CHAPTER 25

Rex's stomach plummeted like a rock to the bottom of an abyss. He was stunned into silence by her words. Closing his eyes against the horror, he fought to keep in control of himself. He took a deep breath and let it out slowly. The extent that Jess had gone to keep her where he wanted her was nothing he'd had to deal with before. It shook him to his core at the viciousness that some people possessed. This was his job. This is what he had wanted to do from the beginning was to protect people like Katy, and now, after seeing it first hand, he knew his compassion for victims of violence would never be lacking.

Katy's hollow voice whispered through the darkness, like smoke from the fire, drifting into the shadows. It pained her to relive each agonizing event and the misery so evident on her brothers face only made the dull ache that'd been dormant so long come back to life. She paused the tumble of words coming from her mouth, chewing her bottom lip, fighting the deep depression that threatened to engulf her. She was safe now. Jess was in hell where he belonged and her beloved brother was there to take her home, well at least she could go home after her jail time was up.

Soft light flittered through the windows leaving lengthening shadows behind. Katy opened her eyes with a start, suddenly aware she was in a strange place. Glancing quickly around, trying to make her sluggish mind make sense of where she was and what she was doing there, a dark shape emerged from a corner toward her.

Like a rock slide, she remembered what had happened to her. Jess, his wicked smile, the cold steel kiss of his gun. Pale Moon, her potions, her cabin. The immense waves of pain, the baby. The baby. The pain was gone now, and so was her baby. It didn't matter that the baby was being born to a vicious man who beat her, or that she hadn't wanted to be trapped by it. It was still hers. A small little person she could teach how to treat people right. A companion she could share her long, lonely days and nights with. She tried to swallow the lump in her throat as the dark shape moving toward her turned into a woman.

"Don't think about it. Just rest." The quiet words spoken by Pale Moon as she moved beside the bed seemed to be reading her tumultuous thoughts. A cool hand on her forehead brushed her loose strands back from her face just like Ma used to do when she was a scared child. Oh how she wished Ma was with her now. Tears sprung unbidden to her eyes. She tried to blink them away, but it was no use. They slid silently down her cheeks and onto the pillow.

"It was best for everyone. Now, you must rest. Your body needs to mend. Drink this."

"Best for who? You! You witch! You're nothin' but a pawn of the devil himself!" The words meant to be screamed came out barely more than a whisper.

"I only did as I was asked, and you know he wouldn't have hesitated to shoot me too. Now drink this. It will help you sleep." Pale Moon's voice stayed calm and soothing as she held the small bowl in one hand and gently lifted Katy's head with the other.

Katy didn't have the strength to shake her head or fight her off. Maybe if she asked Pale Moon to make a potion that would kill her and end her misery, she wouldn't have to feel like this anymore. Just as soon as that thought came, she remembered her oath of vengeance on Jess and Pale Moon. Yes, she would live for revenge.

With mild trepidation, she drank from the proffered bowl. First she needed to regain her strength. Let this horrid woman nurse her back to health, then she would take her revenge.

The next time Katy opened her eyes, darkness had claimed the little cabin, only the faint hint of moon light danced before her eyes. Strange dreams had plagued her, though she couldn't remember them with her eyes open, only the eerie effect they'd had on her lingered. She needed to find her family again and make sure they were safe. The thought hit her as strange, but before she could even try to make sense of it all, her eye lids fell and sleep washed gently over her.

Smells that seemed somewhat familiar tickled her senses and tugged at her closed eyes. Someone was cooking. Her grumbling stomach forced her eyes open, as she lay there debating on whether or not to awaken. Across the small room Pale Moon moved silently and methodically around the kitchen area. A glance at the fireplace confirmed Katy's senses of food. She couldn't see what was being made, but there was the evidence.

For the first time since her ordeal, Katy realized Jess wasn't around. She wasn't sure if this was a good sign or if it meant trouble. She lay there motionless wondering about Jess's absence when Pale Moon turned.

"You're awake. Good. I've made you food to begin getting your strength built back up."

Katy blinked wondering if that's all the strength she had was for that one simple movement. Her entire body felt as if it'd been beaten, the emptiness of her stomach was amplified by the absence of her child. She'd only begun to think her feelings were numb, but at the thought of her child and what they'd done to it, tears threatened to spill from her very soul. She wanted to ask about Jess, just to see if he'd finally abandoned her, but the lump in her throat and the tears welling in her eyes kept her from speaking.

After pouring some liquid into a wooden bowl, Pale Moon came and sat on the side of the bed.

"Today is only broth. Tomorrow will be pieces of meat in your broth, but if we rush it you will be here longer than you want." The dark obsidian eyes that veiled all thoughts seemed to look directly through her own light blue ones Katy thought as Pale Moon helped shift her into a position that would allow her to drink the broth.

The dull clopping of horse hooves slunk through the small cabin's walls. Katy came alert. She rushed to the window to peer out. A whirlwind of mixed emotions assailed her. Her stomach had been in knots since Pale Moon had made her bathe and told her she was going home today. Jess dismounted next to where Pale Moon stood. The last two weeks had almost been relaxing under the ministrations of the dark woman who moved like a silent shadow.

Pale Moon had insisted white women were weaker than Indian women, therefore Katy had been forced to stay in bed until two days ago even though she'd felt relatively normal. After realizing the futility of begging early on, Katy had waited till Pale Moon walked outside before she carefully climbed out of bed and walked quietly around the small cabin knowing that gaining her strength back as quickly as possible was the first step in taking her vengeance on Jess. Katy suspected Pale Moon knew she'd snuck out of bed despite her instructions, but she'd not said a word. The woman seemed to know everything she did and every thought that crossed her mind. It was eerie.

As the voices grew more discernible with the approaching footsteps, Katy's anxiety increased. Pale Moon's cabin had almost seemed somewhat of a refuge for her. Jess hadn't stepped foot in the house after the day he'd brought her here. She'd thought to ask several times, but with the elusive Pale Moon she'd finally let it go knowing he'd return for both of them.

Would he continue to beat her now after what he'd forced her to do? Probably. Nothing had stopped him then, nothing would stop him now.

Hanging her head, she trudged back to sit on the bed. The door opened and sunlight tumbled in behind Jess and Pale Moon.

"Pale Moon says you're well enough to ride again." Jess said as way of greeting.

Katy nodded but kept her eyes lowered, afraid to look into his eyes. Afraid she'd lose her nerve to fight back. Afraid her raw emotions would be self evident.

"Well get goin'. Ain't got all day woman." Motioning toward the door, Jess walked toward her as if to enforce his orders. An inaudible sigh escaped her lips as she stood. Weakness was no longer an option.

Pausing in front of Pale Moon, Katy glanced up at the other woman. For a fleeting instance she thought Pale Moon looked timid. Katy knew her care had not been of her choosing, but not once had Pale Moon shown any hatred toward her. A strange sort of bond had formed between them, a commonality that they understood one another. They were both prisoners of Jess's abuse.

A look of something akin to pity crossed Pale Moon's face as their eyes met. The words Katy had wanted to say, to tell Pale Moon she really didn't hate her, lodged in her throat and she walked out the door.

CHAPTER 26

"Can you believe I actually kinda felt sorry for the woman who helped do that to me?" Katy asked turning her smoky blue eyes to Rex. A half smirk, half grimace turned the corner of her lips. "She has no family. She's a castaway. Durin' that two weeks in her cabin, she only broke once and she didn't say much jus' that the only reason Jess hung on to her was that *once his possession always his possession.* Her mother was raped by a white man, then when she was born her mother disowned her. A medicine woman from a neighboring tribe raised her. Can you imagine?"

Rex didn't bother answering her question. She didn't really expect an answer. He wouldn't have been able to answer if he'd tried. The hatred that had boiled inside him at Jess threatened to explode from every limb of his body. He just stared into the fire, fighting to control his anger. He couldn't do much now anyway with Jess dead. Pale Moon was only a pawn, harmless and not really a criminal threat.

Cracking his knuckles in his hands, Rex wished Katy would finish her story so he could go after the rest of the gang and do something with Jess's body before it started attracting more trouble in the form of coyotes or wolves. The metallic smell of blood had penetrated the air even through the smoke of the fire. He needed to channel his anger into action. This nightmare couldn't end soon enough.

"After that everything went back to jus' like it'd been before. The only difference is that I no longer relied on the whiskey. I knew it made me weak even though it gave me false courage, but I'd finally figured out how to use my fear to build my strength."

"Jess didn't waste any time plannin' the next holdup. He'd actually started plannin' one before he found out about..." she swallowed around a lump starting in her throat, "about the baby, but he wanted to make sure I was with him when they went so he'd put it off. The next hold up we went on was when we held up your stage coach."

Glancing at her brother she looked for the reassurance she so badly needed. He didn't respond to her, instead he sat there staring menacingly into the fire as if he could absorb the flames and hold onto them until he had an opportune time to unleash them on his enemies. For a moment, she wondered if she'd finally snapped and was beginning to lose her mind at the image flashing through her thoughts.

For the thousandth time since Rex had arrived, she reminded herself that she was safe and there was nothing else to fear.

"I have to admit when I saw you three days ago I could barely believe my eyes. I think I almost cried actually. I knew my time to act was here and if I didn't, I'd lose my chance to escape." Hope was beginning to fill her words. Life began to glow from somewhere deep within. She was not dead. She was no long numb. She had survived.

"I'm ashamed I didn't even recognize you until I walked up to you with gun drawn tonight. It took me a little while after the hold up to realize Jess was one of the bandits. I found a horse and took off after him as fast as I could because I knew he'd lead me to you." Rex said turning from the fire. The anger he'd held so tightly to control had began to ebb away.

"It's ok. We're together again and that's all that matters." Katy said matter-of-factly.

"There's only one thing that you haven't told me though. How did you finally pull the trigger?" Rex asked still troubled that his sister who'd gone through so much and who'd been so afraid of the man for so long had finally pulled the trigger on him so calmly.

"Oh you must think I'm horrid." Burying her face in her hands in a gesture of mortification, Katy began to feel the impact of her actions. Her hands shook as she held them away from her face to study them, wondering where the courage had come from to finally end Jess's reign of terror.

"I... I killed him didn't I?" Her body began to shake almost uncontrollably. Standing up and pulling Katy up alongside him, Rex looked directly into her eyes.

"Katy. No one will blame you for what you did. Judge Parker is a fair man. The trial may be rough, but I can assure you after the judge hears what happened, you won't hang."

"I hadn't thought of that. Oh Rex, I was so desperate! Every day we rode away from you was one more day you might lose our trail. One more day to lose hope. I couldn't bare it any more. Everything boiled over at once tonight. I told Jess how bad he was for robbing stages, for beatin' me, for everything. He acted like I was a ravin' lunatic and ignored me. I told him you would find him and kill him! I thought for sure I could provoke him to hit me and it would be enough to warrant me shooting him, but he wouldn't take the bait. For the first time, he didn't hit me, but I was so angry. That's when I went to the saddle bag and dug out the gun he'd given me for emergencies. I wasn't sure if I could really shoot him or not. I thought maybe if I could just scare him enough that he'd at least hold some regard for me and not laugh off my troubles, that if you didn't find me things might improve. But, well, as I stood there with the gun, I automatically pulled back the hammer, and the next thing I knew I was pullin' the trigger." Katy blinked as she stayed focused on Rex's steady gaze. It kept her shaking under control and pried the words from her mouth.

"It was so strange. I felt like I was watchin' someone else pull the trigger. Then you were there before I had a chance to fully realize what I'd done."

"Katy, Katy, Katy." Rex's strong arms pulled her close to him as he murmured her name over and over again in anguish. It felt so good that someone really cared that she fell completely apart all over again. Her strength dissipated and she went limp, sinking softly to the ground where Rex lowered her.

"What's next?" Katy asked as she stood, straightened her shirt, and brushed the dirt from her clothes.

Rex eyed her carefully, measuring her stability. "Next we bring in the rest of the gang."

"We?"

"Yes, we. Me and you. You know these men and how they work. I know you're not goin' anywhere without me so you're gonna help.

A flicker of trepidation crossed Katy's mind. She hadn't actually talked to Pete since the last time he'd been to the cabin and he'd refused to help her run away. He'd been along on the holdup, but neither had attempted to speak to the other. Her mind told her to forget him and not worry about him going to jail, but her heart told her differently.

Fingers of grey tinged with pinks and yellows stretched across the sky. The air hadn't cooled too much and only faint touches of dew lingered. Katy rolled over and realized her mistake. From the tree directly in front of her Jess's body hung suspended by a rope. Her feelings of comfort threatened to flee as she stared at the body. Rex had insisted they couldn't leave the body for the wolves and had managed to pull Jess up into the tree, tying him there. It'd taken some dragging of the body to get him to a tree with a big enough limb, but Rex had done it while Katy had watched in morbid silence.

She was half tempted to untie the rope that was secured around the next tree's base and watch his worthless body come crashing to the ground, but she decided Ma wouldn't be so willing to take her back if she disrespected the dead.

Where was Rex anyway? She turned away from the body to look for her brother. Wisps of smoke from the untended fire floated lazily along on the humid air. She wrinkled her nose as the smell of blood and death processed into her head. Getting up, she didn't waste time starting to pack in her bedroll and other things. She was ready to go.

Muted footsteps in the soft dirt, made Katy whirl around, giving her a start. Rex stood there, covered in dirt. She didn't need to ask where he'd been.

"How are you this mornin'?" He asked as he walked up and hugged her.

"I'm ready to go."

"Sure. Give me a few more minutes." His lanky frame retreated to the tree and released the rope, slowly lowering Jess's body to the ground. Katy stood frozen and watched, still not believing she was finally done with her nightmare.

A few minutes later, Katy stared at the tracks Jess's boots had made as Rex had dragged him to his grave. She heard rocks softly clunking together as Rex covered the shallow grave to protect it from the wolves who howled all night, angry at being cheated out of a meal. The sound of the rocks was somehow comforting. It was the sound of finality.

With her back straight, she mounted her mare and took the reins of Jess's horse patiently waiting for Rex.

Looking outside for the fiftieth time, Katy wondered how long it'd be until the first one showed up and who it would be. Turning from the window she looked behind her, Rex sat alert and calm.

All she'd done was pace since they'd arrived back at the cabin she'd called home for so many months. Walking past Rex, drawing strength from his presence, she made her circle and walked back toward the window.

The other men were supposed to show up tonight. It'd been the plan. Jess had always made sure that at least something from a hold up made it back. After the gang split, a carrier was assigned to each two man team that left together so if anything should happen to one, the others could share in what made it back. It would take the bringing in of the others easy enough, that is if no one got spooked. She restrained from peeking out the window again to see if any of them had rode in unheard.

The first of the dark shadows began to tickle the door of the cabin when Katy finally heard the tell tale sounds of a horse approaching. Her nerves were suddenly jumbled and twisting all together. Who was coming? Would they try to shoot their way out of the trap? She wrung her hands together.

A knock sounded on the wooden door echoing through the cabin in an ominous warning.

Rex raced to his position on feet as silent as the wind. On unsteady legs, Katy walked to the door and opened it.

A rock dropped into her stomach as the blue eyes that stood behind the door locked with hers. For a fleeting second she was tempted to tell Pete to run, but knew it'd be no use. Rex was watching every move.

"Katy." Pete breathed, clearly not expecting her to open the door. An emotion she couldn't place crossed his face for a brief seconds.

"Hands up." Rex ordered as he rounded the door jam, gun drawn on Pete. "Quick inside."

Surprise plastered itself over Pete's face as he looked down the short barrel of Rex's Colt. His hands went into the air as he stepped over the threshold into the dimly lit cabin. Katy opened her mouth to speak but thought better of it.

"Sit." Rex ordered Pete. "You're under arrest for robbery. A formal list of charges will be wrote up later."

"Who are you and where is Whitey?" Pete asked.

"I'm U.S. Deputy Marshal Rex Redfern, Katy's brother. And you are?"

"Pete. Whitey already shackled? Or you already shot him?" Rex glanced at Katy who stood anxiously by the window still wringing her hands. This was supposed to be the least resistant of the men he was arresting on account of her. She clearly wasn't ready to deal with him. Only then did Rex notice she hadn't mentioned Pete at the end of her story. Were they still not speaking?

"Jess is dead. Katy shot him." Pete's mouth gaped open at Rex's revelation.

"It's a lie! You can't pin that on her. She'd never have the guts to do a thing like that!" Pete burst out.

"It's the truth Pete. Rex saw the whole thing. I couldn't take it anymore. You don't know what's happened to me the last couple months." Katy's eyes pleaded with him for understanding. "Rex says the judge will go easy on me after all I've been through. He doesn't think I'll hang."

"You can't make her do that! What'll become of her! That judge don't care. He'll see her hang for sure."

"Don't worry 'bout her. Judge Parker's a fair man. I've been in court plenty lately. You could testify for her as far as what you know the kind of man Jess to have been and help her that way." Rex calmly told him.

Rex heard Pete mutter something under his breath about how he should have killed Jess first and how could a brother take in his own sister. If Pete only knew how hard it was for him to be taking his own sister in in the first place he'd shut his mouth.

"Look Pete. I don't like this any more than you, but I could really use your cooperation in this. The rest of you will get off with a couple years jail time and hopefully we won't have to meet like this again. Now can you sit here and behave while we wait for the others? Otherwise I'll have to get nasty and I don't want to get nasty."

"Pete, please. I asked Rex to take me back with him. I want to go home. I can't take it out here anymore."

"It still ain't right, but looks like I have no choice in the matter." Pete remained motionless as Rex quickly tied his hands with a length of rope then relieved him of his sidearm before returning to his view of the window.

Walking over to where Pete sat, Katy waited for him to look up and meet her eyes. Placing a hand on his, she squatted beside him.

"Thanks for everythin' Pete. I appreciate your tryin' to help me." His only reply was a scowl. She turned away from him and took up her position again, waiting to see who would show up next.

Silence engulfed the cabin as shadows grew longer at every blink of the eye. Rex was lost in thought wondering if he was doing the right thing when a warm breath on his neck raised his hairs to danger a fraction of a second before he felt the barrel of a gun against his ribs.

"Listen to me." At Pete's soft menacing voice behind Rex, Katy spun to face the two men, her hand clasp over her mouth at the sight of Pete's bound hands holding one of Rex's own Colts on him. Rex raised his hands, the other gun still in his grip. "When we get to Fort Smith you're goin' to tell the judge that I shot Whitey not Katy."

"I can't do that Pete." The hard barrel pressed further into his ribs.

"You tell the judge that or you can start countin' your last breaths. I shoulda shot that bastard long time ago when Katy first told me what he was, but I was too afraid then, but I'm not afraid now. She can't even count on her own brother to protect her so it's my job to make sure she doesn't take the blame for killin' a man. You know she'll be ruined for good if she's labeled a murderer, even if it was for self preservation."

"Pete, don't do this, please." Katy pleaded from where she stood a few yards away.

"Katy, I failed you too many times. I'm not gonna do it again. You saved my life once, now it's my turn to repay that debt."

"It won't work, Pete. You weren't even there." Rex said calmly, the gun in his hand useless as it aimed skyward above his head.

"I say it will. Here's how I see it. Since I knew of Whitey's character, I circled around after we split to check on Katy. I confronted him and after exchangin' words, I shot him in a fit of rage."

"Pete, don't worry about. I'll be fine." Katy tried again.

"We do it my way or I shoot you right here and now."

"You wouldn't shoot me. I'm her brother. She'd hate you for that." Rex tried to call Pete's bluff only to hear the sound of the hammer being cocked.

"She can hate me, but she ain't gonna hang for shootin' Whitey. Not after what she's been through."

"What if I agree now, but then I tell the judge the truth? And add threatening a deputy with intent to kill to your charges." Rex asked.

"I will find you and I will kill you." Pete said simply.

Katy bit her finger as the two men in her life tried to call the other's bluff in the name of protecting her and finding justice. She wanted to scream, but if she did she might ruin the chances for Rex to catch the others if they heard her.

Exhaling a frustrated sigh, Rex consented to Pete's demands. As soon as Rex had agreed, Pete withdrew the Colt, replacing it in Rex's holster then took a step back. No sooner had the firearm been replaced to its holster, than Rex whipped around, his arm still raised with his other Colt high the air.

Without thinking, Katy rushed up to Rex and caught his hand just as he went to bring it down and pistol whip Pete.

"Stop it! Stop it! I'm so sick of the violence. Please stop it!" Katy fought control of her voice.

Slowly Rex's arm lowered. Pete walked backward to his chair, neither man taking his eyes off the other. Rex was about to go for another length of rope to tie Pete into the chair when the sound of another horse approaching reached the inside of the cabin.

CHAPTER 27

Holding her breath, Katy watched out of the corner of the window, waiting to see who would show up next. On the other side of the window Rex stood as poised as a cat ready to pounce. Katy wondered if he was even breathing. Her racing heart pounded in her ears, the silence was overwhelming.

A horse and rider appeared at the edge of the woods, a short expanse across the small yard. It was Rick. Katy felt a sinking feeling deep in her gut. Rick was one of the most dangerous. If Rex wasn't careful this would end badly.

Rick's horse had only taken a few steps into the yard when it bobbed its head and nickered. Rick's head popped up alert. Katy risked a glance at Rex. He hadn't taken his eyes off Rick, but she felt his muscles tense. Craning her neck around farther to look back at Pete, Katy studied him. He sat quietly, head bowed, as if resigned to his fate. A pang of strong emotion coursed through her as the realization of what he was willing to do finally hit her. He wanted to be hanged for murder in her place even though she was the one who'd pulled the trigger.

Suddenly, Katy was jerked from her thoughts as a faint breeze from movement near her brushed past, the thundering of boots on the wood floor echoing in the silence.

"Hold the house till I get back! Try not to shoot anybody." Rex called over his shoulder as he raced for the door.

Katy whipped around to the window to see what had happened. Out of the corner of her eye she saw movement as Pete's head came up. The tail of Rick's horse swished into the tree line. He was on the run. A high pitched whistle pierced the air seconds before Rex's horse appeared. In a flash of motion Rex was mounted and quickly disappeared from view.

Slumping against the wall, Katy wished there was a different way.

"Who ran?" Pete's quiet voice carried across the small room.

"Rick."

He nodded as if that explained enough. "If your brother loses him he'll disappear for good. No one will be able to find him if he gets away."

Turning back to the window, Katy wondered if she even cared if Rick was caught. She had no personal feeling toward him. He'd only looked at her with distain, but never said an unnecessary word to her, or touched her like Clay. Rick was just there as Jess's right hand. Straightening her shoulders, she hoped Rex caught him. Being the devil's right hand was bad enough.

As the silence dragged on, unease filled her mind. What would happen if the others showed up? Morgan and Clay were still due here. Would Rick kill Rex in his escape attempt? Looking at her hands, she realized she'd been wringing them together in nervousness again.

It seemed as if her fears were walking, breathing, living things. No sooner had the doubts began to assail her mind than the sounds of another horse approaching reached her ears. It was only one horse she was sure. If it was only Rex he'd lost Rick, but somehow she didn't think he'd give up so soon. No, it was one of the others. She needed a gun.

The hunting rifle still hung above the fire place. Racing across the room, Katy quickly got it down to load it. She could feel Pete's eyes follow her around, but he sat silently. By the time she had the gun ready the rider had dismounted and was walking up to the door.

Taking a deep breath, she tried to steady her nerves before she faced whoever was on the other side. Reaching out her hand to open the door, she decided the element of surprise needed to be on her side.

Hinges groaned in protest as the door began to open, but before it had swung completely back, Katy had the butt of the rifle to her shoulder and was looking down the barrel at a very stunned Clay.

His cold blue eyes were wide in shock, his mouth worked, but no sound came at first.

"What the hell?" He finally managed to ask.

"Get in the house." Katy spoke, her voiced sounding stronger than she felt. She stepped back letting him in.

As Katy circled around Clay, she kicked the door shut. Clay caught sight of Pete sitting quietly in the chair, hands bound in his lap.

"Pete, what's goin' on? Has she lost her mind?" Clay's questions stopped as Pete glared at him.

"Shut up." Pete told him, his words punctuated by the shutting of the door behind Clay.

Keeping the rifle trained on Clay, she moved him forward. Just as they took their first step a sound outside silenced the room. Another horse was coming into the clearing.

"You make one sound and I will shoot you." Katy said quietly behind Clay.

"Where's Whitey?" Clay demanded.

"I shot him." Pete said before Katy had a chance to answer.

"You what?!" Clay was incredulous.

"Shut up. He can tell you about it later." Katy was getting frantic. She needed to tie Clay up before the other rider reached the house. She didn't have time. Clay seemed to relax as the seconds ticked by, realizing her dilemma offered escape.

"Give me the gun Katy. I'll make sure he doesn't escape." Pete said breaking into her scattered thoughts, motioning to her with his hands to give him the gun. "You just get Morgan in here."

Morgan would run, or help the others escape if she let him go. She looked back at Pete. She had to trust him. He was already taking the fall for her. What other choice did she have?

"What's the matter with you? Have you lost your damn mind?" Clay's voice had raised an octave.

Katy handed the gun to Pete after she made Clay sit in the floor at close range, his back to Pete. For a second she considered untying Pete's hands so he could handle the gun better, but after the little scene between him and Rex it was probably better she didn't.

Where was Rex anyway? What would she do if he didn't come back? She refused to think past that. He would come back. He had to.

"Now you just sit still and quiet, and hope that these ropes don't get tangled in this gun and make it accidently go off." Pete told Clay.

Turning toward the door, Katy wondered how Morgan would react.

Without a weapon in hand, she let Morgan knock on the door before answering it as if it were just a social call.

"How are you Katy?" Morgan greeted, smiling warmly, as she opened the door. He carried one the bags of money and trinkets robbed from the stage in his hands, but her gaze went past that to his waste and noticed he wasn't wearing a gun. He usually kept it in his bags until they were performing one of their jobs, she almost sighed with relief. The fewer guns present, the better this would turn out, she hoped.

"I'm alright. Come in." Her cordiality was almost genuine. She almost liked this rough man who'd sort of been like an uncle to her.

"Am I the last one here again?" He asked her smiling. Pete and Clay sat near the corner out of the direct line of sight behind the door.

"Nearly." He stepped into the room and instantly stilled at he saw Pete holding the rifle on Clay.

"What's going on Katy?" Morgan asked.

"Come sit down." She motioned to the other chair diagonal to Pete. He took a step then stopped as Katy saw his gaze rest on Pete's tied hands.

"Come on Morgan. I won't shoot anybody I don't have to." Pete told him.

Morgan's eyes darted around the small room. The light was dim Katy realized. She needed to light a lamp before they were plunged into total darkness shortly, but first she needed to tie the other two men up.

"Where's Whitey?" Morgan asked after he sat in the chair.

"Dead." Pete answered not taking his eyes off of Clay. Any shock Morgan may have shown was hidden by the shadows crossing the room.

"Rick?"

"Bein' chased by her brother." Katy saw Clay's shoulders slump slightly at Pete's answer.

"Your brother?" Morgan questioned her as she picked up the rope Rex had left behind on the floor and began tying Clay's feet.

"My brother is a U. S. deputy marshal. He was the one on the stage we robbed a few days ago that Jess pointed out."

Silence descended on the room as the implications of that statement sunk in.

"Ginny!" Morgan tried to jump up, as he seemed to suddenly remember her, just as Katy reached him to bind his hands.

"We'll take care of her Morgan. I want to help Ginny."

"What about when you go to jail with the rest of us?"

"My ma or my aunt will take care of her, I'm sure."

Sitting back he hung his head. "What kind of uncle am I anyway? I don't know nothin' bout raisin' no kids. I know I can't do it from jail though. I'm all she's got left."

Pain filled eyes lifted to hers as she finished her knot on his hands.

"Maybe you should think about makin' an honest livin' after you get out." Katy suggested.

"I don't know nothin'. I tried farmin'. I tried blacksmithin'. I can't do it. All I know how to do is rob people."

"We'll figure somethin' out, but Ginny needs you. You gotta go straight." Katy pinned him with her best no nonsense look, but inside she was thinking he looked about as miserable as a man could look.

Taking the rifle back from Pete, she tried to make herself comfortable with the gun resting across her lap and her wondering gaze flashing to the window. Night was closing in fast and Rex was nowhere in sight. She tried to ignore the what-ifs that threatened to turn her into a whimpering child.

Katy had lit every candle she could find before the last shadow had melded into night. Rex had still not returned and she was getting nervous. She'd paced back and forth to the window a thousand times. Pete sat silently, a complete mask of his emotions covered his face. Clay had leered at her as he watched her unease grow. She really wanted to shoot him. It'd been such a relief to shoot Jess. Clay wouldn't be much different. However, the memory of the face of death and the sounds of the blood gurgling from Jess's mouth had kept her from taking her agitation out on Clay. Justice. Justice. She rehearsed inwardly to herself over and over. She wouldn't have an alibi if she shot Clay either. Morgan would witness against her and Rex wouldn't let her get away with two murders no matter what Pete threatened.

The door creaked behind Katy. She jumped and whirled around. She'd been so engrossed in her own thoughts she'd failed to listen for any one approaching.

Two shadows appeared in the doorway. The taller one shoved the other inside. Rick's face glowered with hatred as his face fell into the light as he stumbled forward.

Breathing a sigh of relief, she bounded from her perch to her brothers side. She wanted to hug him and feel his strength and reassurance, but she held back not wanting to distract him until he was ready.

"We've been waitin' for you to join this lil shindig." Clay said sarcastically as Rick fell on the floor beside him after losing his balance with his hands bound behind his back.

If eyes could commit murder, the look Rick gave Clay would have been a dagger to his heart. Rex bent down and righted his prisoner before taking in the other two that had been assembled in his absence.

As Rex informed each of his prisoners they were formally under arrest, Katy saw the blood and bruising on Rick. Dirt and small sticks clung haphazardly to his clothing and hair. Turning her gaze on her brother she realized he was only in slightly better shape. A cut on his lower lip had a small drop of blood showing, the lip looked like it was swelling and a red spot glowed from his cheek bone about the size of a fist. Rex's clothes were only slightly less dirty and no sticks dangled from his short hair.

Katy wrapped her arms around Rex as soon as he finished speaking. He squeezed her back.

"You did good sis." He said softly in her ear.

"I've been so scared. I'm so glad you're back and you're safe." She felt the pull of tears threatening her eyes.

"I'm here now. Tomorrow we'll go home."

Home. Her home. She smiled. It felt good to think about home. No loose ends. No worries.

"Wait. We can't go until we get Ginny." Katy told him.

"The lil girl you told me about right?"

"Yes. She's home alone tonight, probably scared out of her mind."

Rex looked at the four prisoners and then back to his sister. "We'll go get her on our way out in the mornin'. It's too late to go after her tonight."

She thought about protesting, but saw the logic of his decision.

CHAPTER 28

Ginny's small hand gripped Katy's tighter as they followed the four prisoners and Rex onto the ferry that would take them across the Arkansas River. This was the first indication Ginny had given of being afraid since the morning they'd come to take her away from the only place she felt safe.

For the hundredth time, Katy hoped against hope that Judge Parker wouldn't give her a long sentence for her deeds so she could return to care for Ginny. She was certain Ma and Aunt Stella would be happy to care for her in the mean time, but she felt responsible for the small girl. Maybe it was because they shared a common bond of loss and tragedy. They'd lived in the same kind of life full of fear.

Together at the rail, the two of them watched the muddy waters of the Arkansas pass beneath them wondering what life held for them on the other side of the river. Rex stood off to the side as secluded as he could get on the crowded ferry with his prisoners. Katy wished she could read their thoughts, but each man's face was a mask.

"What's your ma like?" Ginny's small voice broke into Katy's thoughts. The girl's blue eyes were like saucers. The fears of newness clear on her small face. Katy knelt down on one knee next to Ginny. She still wore the men's clothes she'd become so accustomed to wearing. Besides she'd ripped up her old dress for rags long ago and the fancy dresses Jess had bought her made travelling harder, not to mention the bad memories they conjured up in her mind. However, she'd brought the dresses along, but was still unsure of what she would do with them. Ma would throw a ring-tailed fit when she saw the clothes she wore, but she thought she could handle Ma's wrath over her clothes easier than the nightmare.

"You'll like her. She's very nice. She likes to cook and she makes the best biscuits. She's lonely and would love to have somebody to keep her company."

"Do you think she'll like me?"

"I know she will." Katy tousled the little girl's feathery blonde hair; the wind caught it and tossed it higher. The glow of the sun behind her head made the small girl look almost angelic. There was no way Ma would turn this little girl away Katy thought.

"I see you caught them." The voice came from beside the ragtag group nearing the jail.

"Yes sir. It's a long story, but you'll have it as soon as I get them locked up and my report in." Rex addressed the voice.

Katy and Ginny had been walking behind the men, she now peered around her brother to see who he'd spoken to. The man wore a badge. She didn't see much past the shiny star pinned to his chest. If Rex was reporting to him, this must be the marshal. She must've tightened her grip on Ginny's hand because the little girl started to squirm. Their horses had been left at the livery near the dock when they'd exited the ferry. Rex's theory was that it was less likely for any of them to make a run for it on foot now that their fate seemed so imminent.

"By the way Rattlesnake, you didn't happen to cross paths with Chip out there did you?"

"No. Were we supposed to?" The group had come to a stop near the marshal.

"Not particularly so. His partner came in yesterday from the Territory and seemed to think he should've been here. They'd been sent after a band of horse thieves, but his partner claims he came down with a serious bout of stomach trouble and Chip insisted he needed to go on without him. He was laid up for several day before he tried to catch back up with Chip, but he didn't find any sign of him so he came back thinkin' he'd already made it back here. Nobody's seen or heard from him in a few weeks." The marshal stopped and looked behind Rex, as if seeing Katy and Ginny for the first time.

Katy looked down feeling embarrassed. Rex followed the marshal's gaze.

"I found my sister Katy out there too. It'll all be in my reports after I lock these men up." Rex said turning back to the marshal.

The marshal nodded. "Carry on."

As Katy stepped into the shadow of the brick building that housed the jail, an ominous feeling settled over her. It could've been from the case of nerves she'd had since that morning, or the fact that she'd had to face the judge and also testify against the others. Either way she wasn't sure she could stomach the stench that emanated from the window, wafting into her sense. She held Ginny back at the door while Rex directed the men inside.

Rex paused in the doorway before closing the door behind him. "I'll see if they'll let me be your guard at home until trial. Wait here until I come back out."

Large blue eyes with strands of blonde hair scattered across them peered up at her. "Katy, what's gonna happen to Uncle Morgan?"

No matter how hard she'd tried to explain to Ginny, the question remained would he be released one day to come back to her and take her home.

"He'll have to go before the judge and tell him what he did and why. Then he'll have to tell him about you. Judge Parker will tell your Uncle Morgan how long he has to stay here before he lets him free again. When that happens, we'll know how long it will be until you can go with him again, but until then you can stay with us." Katy hesitated. Well she was about to be locked up with the rest with only Rex and Ma to look out for Ginny. "Don't worry Rex isn't really mean. He jus' looks it."

Tears threatened again. How could she tell this small girl how good her brother really was? That all he wanted in life was to keep people safe from the wolves that preyed on the innocent. That her own uncle had been one of those wolves. And that she, Katy, had also been a preying wolf, selfish and self absorbed until she'd seen the truth. It was almost too much for her to take in, let alone explain to this innocent child who only needed the love of a family. Katy blinked the tears away before she let them fall.

Ginny just nodded her head. Katy could see the questions and uncertainty in her eyes. Without thinking she wrapped her arms around the thin shoulders and drew her close. The soft wispy yellow hair tickled her nose.

"I'm gonna tell Rex to stop and buy you a piece of candy on the way out to Ma's place."

They were still seated on the steps outside the jail when Rex walked out, blinking in the bright light.

"I need to walk over and talk to Judge Parker for a minute about ya'll. Be back in a few minutes."

Katy watched her lanky brother's retreating form as he walked across the small square yard to the judge's quarters that sat catty-corner to the jail. He really was a handsome man. Why couldn't he find a woman and settle down? It would do him good. The answer was obvious though. He held his job in higher regard than he ever would a woman.

As she sat there pondering her brother's lonely life, the same thoughts turned inward. Would she ever find a man to truly love? Was she now forever ruined after her little foray into Indian Territory?

The more she thought about it the more bleak her future looked. Her mood turned more morose by the minute. Why did Pete have to go and do such a fool thing as play the murderer? He should've let her pay for her crimes. The result would've been death within the next few months, with only minimal suffering or a life in prison where she wouldn't have to worry about life outside. As it was her future looked as grim as the dark and dreary prison walls behind her.

By the time Rex returned from his talk with the judge, Katy's mood was dark and brooding.

"Alright," Rex placed a booted foot on the steps where Katy and Ginny still sat, leaning his elbow on his knee, "I've outlined our problem to Judge Parker and he's allowed that since we don't have good facilities for women, he'll release you to me until your trial. However, that also means I'm grounded from leavin' town until the trial is over too."

"Sorry." Katy grumbled her half hearted apology. Why'd he have to leave again anyway? Couldn't the marshal and the judge find some job for him to do here?

"The other catch is that you can't be seen off our property. If you are, you may have to face more charges." Rex's blue eyes pinned her with the seriousness of the situation, but they softened almost as quickly. "I know you're not a real criminal, but it's easy for those who don't know you to wag their tongues and make trouble."

"Got it. No trouble." Katy mumbled, as she looked down at her boots. Maybe no one would recognize her if she kept dressing like a man, then nobody could blame her for anything.

"Ginny, you ready to go meet mine and Katy's ma?" Rex turned his attention to the little girl who's arm was linked through Katy's, clinging tightly in fear, and smiled.

Ginny seemed to relax only slightly as Rex smiled for the first time at her.

"I told her you'd buy her a piece of candy on the way out of town," Katy told Rex as they stood up to leave.

"Of course I will." Reaching out a hand to her, Rex took the small, timid hand that slowly stretched out to him, in his larger ones. "Let's go see what ol' Mrs. Lindsey has for you today."

CHAPTER 29

The road, that was really no more than a weedy wagon path slashed through the woods, felt so familiar, yet somehow seemed like a different world. The whole countryside was awash in greens, yellows, and every conceivable color of flower that grew native to the area. Katy had seen little of the familiar vegetation in the Territory; everything there had seemed so barren and lifeless. Had it only been the season she was there?

Her heart squeezed in her chest as the little cabin she'd spent most of her life in came into view. She pulled on the reigns slowing her mare's easy trot to slow walk. Ginny slowed to her pace. Rex's horse picked up its pace, its white feet dancing across the ground as if it knew it was home. The journey was over.

A moment later Ma walked to the open door of the cabin. Katy watched as Rex dismounted and walked into Ma's waiting arms. As her horse slowly inched forward, she could tell Rex was telling Ma about her. Ma stilled as her gaze swung to the two approaching horses.

"Katy! Katy!" Katy watched as Ma ran full out toward her. Katy's mare tossed its head at the sight of the running woman yelling at them. Quieting the horse she tightened the reign and stopped it. Without thinking, she was out of the saddle and had barely turned when Ma caught her in a stifling embrace.

"Oh Katy, you're alive! I've been so worried. I've missed you." Ma pulled back enough to look at Katy's face. She reached up, wiping a tear that streaked down, glistening in the sunlight. Drops of happiness streamed down her face.

"I've missed you too." The words found their way out despite the lump in her throat. She couldn't help but wonder if Ma would feel so warmly toward her after she told her the story of her time in the Territory. Just that thought kept some of the joy out of their reunion.

Suddenly she remembered Ginny. Katy twisted toward Ginny who sat atop her horse, watching the exchange between mother and daughter with a look of wistfulness.

"Ma this is Ginny. Can you help care for her for a while?"

"Of course." Ma said, giving Katy a look that said she knew there was a story behind the girl that shouldn't be discussed in front of her.

Rex had caught up to the group and gone past the women to Ginny. He reached up, lifting Ginny from her saddle, and set her gently on the ground. She gave him a shy, timid smile.

As they all walked toward the cabin Katy couldn't help but wonder how long she'd have to enjoy home before being locked away.

Only one candle was left burning hours after Rex and Ginny had succumbed to sleep. Katy had poured out her hurt and troubles to Ma. By the time she had finished her story for the second time within a week she was emotionally spent. She sagged against Ma, her eyes puffy and burning from all the spent tears that had ceased hours ago. Her body had no strength left to keep her upright. Leaning against Ma, she tried to draw from her strength, but she knew Ma had little to give. She'd seen the wrinkles that had deepened in Ma's brow since she'd left home. The streaks of grey in her hair seemed wider and greyer. Ma had aged years in the last eight months. Katy knew it was her fault, but now that she was back she intended to make everything right. She would be the model daughter, as long as she wasn't locked away in jail.

The next morning men's voices penetrated Katy's foggy mind. She felt something shift beneath her head. Turning to move, aches assailed her body from neck to legs. Squinting against the light pouring through the windows, she realized she still sat in a chair in the living room.

It all came crashing back to her as the wiggle next to her persisted. She and Ma had fallen asleep together sometime in the deep darkness of night. Ma's comforting arms had lulled her into a peaceful sleep. Neither must have moved the entire night as the pain in Katy's neck attested to the poor position of her head.

Sitting up, Katy stretched every muscle she could to make sure it still worked. Glancing over at Ma, she saw she was in much worse condition. Ma had tried to stand right after Katy moved from her shoulder, now she walked hunchbacked and with a pronounced limp as she made her way to her bedroom.

The buzzing in her ears that had started when she sat upright faded and the voices that had originally awakened her reached her ears again.

Curiosity overruling her better senses, Katy tiptoed to the window and peeked out the side of the curtain. Rex stood talking to a grey haired man that looked like he'd just walked out of the mountains, a few feet from the cabin.

"Katy?" A small voice behind her made her nearly jump. She turned to see Ginny standing in the doorway to her old room, the little girl's hair stood out all askew, a small hand rubbed sleepy eyes.

"Good mornin' Ginny." Katy tiptoed back away from the window as she spoke to the girl. "Would you like to sit in the kitchen while I help Ma prepare some breakfast?"

The blonde head nodded. Katy led her into the
kitchen and pulled out a chair for her to sit. She
immediately started a fire in the iron cook stove.

Comforting heat was seeping from the stove
when Ma walked into the kitchen without a trace of
the rough night she'd spent sleeping in the chair. An
impish smile touched her eyes and made her look
younger than she had the night before. Katy
wondered if it'd only been the light playing tricks
on her eyes.

Sweet smells of home and food were radiating
from the kitchen when Katy heard the door to the
cabin open.

"So you say you're gonna be 'round for a
couple of weeks?" An unfamiliar voice asked as
two sets of boots sounded across the wooden floor
heading in the direction of the kitchen.

Katy cocked her head to listen, wondering who
Rex was talking too. It was no one she recognized.
She looked to Ma for a hint and what she saw made
her pause. Ma was actually beaming! Beaming like
a school girl.

"Yeah I'm here till after the hearin'." Rex
answered as the two men appeared in the door way.

"Mornin' Roslin." Katy's mouth dropped open
at hearing Ma's Christian name coming from the
this stranger.

"Mornin' Lee."

"And this must be Katy." The mountain man
named Lee smiled at her, extending his hand as he
crossed the short distance between them. "We've all
been prayin' for your safe return."

Katy's mouth worked, but the words were lost somewhere in her shock at hearing the man say "we" as if he and a dozen others had been praying for her return not to mention the fact he'd used Ma's name. Through her shock, she finally managed to extend a hand to him in return and answer with a feeble "thank you". His strong hand engulfed hers as he clasp her hand, then patted the open top of her hand with the other hand.

The strange man turned to Ginny. "Who do we have here?" His eyes flickered almost unnoticeably to Ma. "I don't believe I know who this young lady is."

"This is Ginny. I'm carin' for her while her uncle awaits his trial, and probably until his jail time is served." Ma said, the smile on her face never wavering.

Katy turned to Rex hoping for some sort of explanation. He winked at her. Had the whole world turned upside down since she'd left?

Lee knelt next to the little girl so he was eye level with her. "Ginny, you couldn't ask for a better woman than Roslin to care for you. She's a great lady with a heart the size of an oak tree." Katy watched as the little girl's timid gaze looked up into the strangers eyes, traces of a smile tugged at the corners of her lips.

"Katy, this is Lee. We're engaged and plan to marry at the end of summer. That is, when your brother decides to stay around long enough for us to have a proper ceremony."

Confusion over took Katy. She couldn't think. What about Pa, he was barely in his grave. Who was this man that had come in trying to take her pa's place so soon? She turned and fled from the room. Voices buzzed behind her, but the words were just a cauldron of noise, nothing discernible in the mix.

Fleeing out the front door, Katy headed to her favorite thinking spot near the creek to sort it all out in her head.

After staring at the creek rushing along for an indeterminable amount of time, soft footsteps approached behind her.

"Katy." Without turning she knew it was Rex. "I know it's a lot to take in your first day home, but in time you'll see how good this is for Ma."

Turning to look up at him, she wondered how he could be so calm and relaxed about it all. The answer was simple. He'd been here and knew what was going on when she hadn't been. He'd had time to adjust, to cope. She looked back to the creek feeling as unsettled as the water rushing past her feet. Without an invitation, Rex sat beside her.

"Give him a chance Katy. He's not tryin' to take Pa's place, but he does make Ma happy."

She didn't know what to think or say, so she said nothing. Together they sat staring into the creek until Rex finally stood.

"It's all gonna turn out alright Katy. I promise." His words were a whisper. She knew he couldn't really promise that it really would turn out okay, especially since most of it was out of his control, but his confidence gave her the beginning thread of hope to cling to.

EPILOGUE

Late May heat was trying its best to squeeze the sweat out of the bricks of the three story structure that housed the criminals from the Western District of Arkansas and Indian Territory, Rex thought as he walked down the dimly lit corridor. The paper he held in his hands weighed him down more than he expected it would. He shouldn't have read it, but when it came to his sister, he found he was a little over protective. He was just glad the trials were over and he had his assignment that would put him back on the trail again.

Katy had only received the minimal sentence of six months for her part in the robberies. The others had a longer stay. Yesterday the verdict had been turned in for Pete. His life would be spared, thanks to the jury's sense of chivalry towards women. If Katy hadn't testified on his behalf, Rex was sure he'd have a summer date with the gallows. His hand clenched the folded paper as he remembered the look on Katy's face as she again described the life she'd lived since she'd left home.

She and Ma had spent half the day before her trial started ironing one of the dresses she'd brought back with her. It'd been the first day of trials that he'd seen she was no longer a child, but a full grown woman. He had no control over her any more. Maybe that's why he felt compelled to actually deliver the letter crumpled in his hands instead of ripping it up and throwing it away.

He stopped at the door to the small room that was barely bigger than a single outhouse. Katy looked up startled from where she sat on the bunk.

"Rex." The look on her face was pitiful. The short time she'd spent in the cell had aged her five years at least already. He could see it in the lines of her eyes and the shape of her mouth that seemed to be set in a frown.

"I have a letter for you and I wanted to tell you I'm headed out into the Territory again. I have to go look for Chip and the gang of horse thieves he was after." He passed the single sheet of paper through the bars.

"Be careful out there. Come see me when you get back."

"I will." He couldn't take it anymore. He quickly whirled around and stalked out the door. He couldn't wait for her to read the letter and watch any more emotion seep from her sweet face.

The stench of the place did nothing to placate him. The words of the letter reverberated with the echoing sound of his boots down the corridor.

Dear Katy,

I can't even begin to tell you how badly I feel for how everything turned out. I should have been a man and taken care of the problem when I had the chance. It shouldn't have fallen on your shoulders. How it ever came to this I don't know if I'll ever fully understand myself. I hope you can find it in your heart to forgive me. I acted the coward, but I want you to know that it will never happen again. You have taught me the consequences of cowardly action.

I hope you are being treated well. I have no right to ask you this, but when I get out in a few years if I find you are still unattached I would like to come calling on you like the gentleman I plan to become.

Yours always,

Pete

Rex lowered his hat as he squinted into the sunlight when he opened the door. A man stopped in front of him.

"Bein' inside that jail is 'bout enough to kill a man's eyesight ain't it?"

"You got that right Marshal." Rex blinked one last time before being able to keep his eyes open.

"Got everythin' ready to head out to the Territory?"

"Yes sir. I jus' had to stop by and see Katy before I left. Meetin' Flint and Lee out by the ferry before it goes back across."

"How's she doin'?"

"As good as can be expected." Rex didn't feel the need to tell this man about the rest of his problems concerning her.

"Terrible what a fella can convince a woman to do." The marshal shook his head as if saddened by Katy's fate. He looked up at Rex and held out his hand as he changed subjects. "Well, I jus' hope you can find Chip and he don't end up like that poor sap we found last August a few miles from the depot across the river that was never identified."

Rex shook hands with the marshal before turning to go. "Me too Marshal. Me too."

ABOUT THE AUTHOR

Jennette Gahlot is an Arkansas Native who has a deep love of history and writing. She is a graduate of Arkansas Tech University. Currently, she has a growing palate of books out ranging from historical fiction to poetry to children's stories.

If you enjoyed this book, write a short review on your favorite online retailer and tell others about it. I also love to hear directly from my readers. You can find me at:
Email: jenpenbooks@gmail.com
www.jennettegahlot.com
facebook: Jennette Gahlot books
twitter: @JennetteGahlot

Thanks for reading!

67081341R00178

Made in the USA
Charleston, SC
04 February 2017